She knew nothing of sexual affinity

Helen was frightened, and yet the pull she felt toward him electrified her.

"I know the name Magnus means great, but I don't think you're well named," she said acidly. "There's nothing great about deceiving a woman and then...to add insult to injury, sexually harassing her!"

Magnus drew back from her as if she had hit him, and his eyes narrowed warily.

"And when have I sexually harassed you?" he demanded.

"You didn't have to kiss me," she argued weakly.

"Agreed," he murmured, moving closer to her.

"I didn't have to. I did it because I couldn't help it," he replied, his voice still soft. "I did it to find out what you're really like behind that act you put on of being a cool, liberated type of woman about to indulge in an affair with another woman's husband."

Books by Flora Kidd

These books may be available at your local bookseller.

For a free catalog listing all titles currently available,
send your name and address to:

Harlequin Reader Service
P.O. Box 52040, Phoenix, AZ   85072-9988
Canadian address: Stratford, Ontario   N5A 6W2

FLORA KIDD

dangerous encounter

Harlequin Books

TORONTO • NEW YORK • LONDON
AMSTERDAM • PARIS • SYDNEY • HAMBURG
STOCKHOLM • ATHENS • TOKYO • MILAN

Harlequin Presents first edition January 1984
ISBN 0-373-10657-2

Original hardcover edition published in 1983
by Mills & Boon Limited

CHAPTER ONE

THE telephone on the desk rang shrilly and demandingly, once, twice, three, four times. There was no one in the office to answer it. On the fifth ring a young woman appeared in a doorway which opened into another room. She was about twenty-two, tall and slim, and her fair straight hair was tied back simply behind her neck to fall in a long silky tail down her back. Over her skirt and blouse she was wearing a white hospital coat, indicating that she was either a doctor or a laboratory technician. Her thin face was not exactly pretty, but her skin was fine and white and her bones were elegantly chiselled. She would blossom into beauty as she grew older.

On the sixth ring of the telephone bell she picked up the receiver.

'Glencross Regional Hospital Laboratory,' she said in a cool briskly professional voice which held just the slightest suspicion of a Scottish accent. 'Helen Melrose speaking.'

Someone at the other end of the line cleared his throat and then a familiar voice, also softened by a Scottish accent, spoke.

'Blair here, Helen. I was hoping I'd reach you first time and not the secretary.'

At the sound of the man's voice Helen's face changed its expression. It became wary and her large tawny-brown eyes narrowed. She bit the corner of her soft pink lower lip with the edge of well-shaped white teeth.

5

'I thought you'd phone me at the flat before this,' she murmured. 'You said you would. Is everything all right? Are we still going away for the weekend?'

'Do you still want to go away . . . with me?'

'I . . . I'd like to go away, but I'm not sure. . . .' she began, but he interrupted her.

'I am. I'm looking forward to being alone with you. I can hardly wait,' he said, his voice deepening with emotion.

Helen's pale cheeks flushed with pink colour betraying her sudden inner excitement. Blair sounded like a man who was desperately in love, and she was glad there was no one in the laboratory office to notice her reaction to his verbal lovemaking.

'All right,' she whispered, 'I'll go away with you. You said on Monday that you'd like to leave this afternoon, about one o'clock. Will you pick me up at the flat?'

'No, I can't do that. Something has come up and I can't get away as soon as I'd hoped. Also I think it would be best if we travel separately. You could go ahead of me and I'll join you later, this evening.'

'But I don't know where we're going,' she reminded him with a laugh. 'You didn't tell me on Monday. You said it was to be a secret until we got there, that you wanted to surprise me.'

'Mmm, I did, didn't I? How romantic of me!' There was a note of mockery in the voice which was unusual, because Blair wasn't disposed to making fun of himself. 'Well, I can't keep it a secret any longer. We're going to stay in a castle on an island off the west coast, not far from Oban.'

'That sounds delightful, but I hope it isn't in ruins.'

'No, it's in pretty good shape. It's been renovated, but it's fairly isolated and that's why I thought it would be a good place for us to stay. Would you mind driving there by yourself?'

'No, not at all. I've never been that way before. And I do agree with you that it would be best if we left here separately without arousing any suspicions.'

'I thought you might.' Again there was a certain dryness in his voice that puzzled her.

'So will you tell me how to get there, please?' Helen asked.

'Of course. It's rather an awkward drive. Go from here across the river to Dumbarton and then take the road along the shore of Loch Long to Arrochar. From Arrochar go west and down Loch Fyne through Inverary to Lochgilphead, then turn north for Oban. When you're about five miles along the Oban road look for a signpost to the village of Ballacuish and follow that road as far as it goes, right to the sea. There's a jetty there and a crofter's cottage.' He paused for a moment, then added, 'Magnus will meet you there. I've told him to expect you. He'll take you over to the island of Carroch in the motorboat.'

'Who is Magnus?' she asked.

'You could say he's the caretaker of the castle.'

'Does he live in it?'

'Er . . . yes.'

'Then he'll be there while we're there. We won't be alone.'

'Do you mind?' asked Blair.

'No, not really.' Actually Helen was quite relieved that there would be other people in the castle. Magnus probably had a wife who was the housekeeper. 'Who owns the castle?'

There was a brief silence and she thought she could hear the sound of music in the background and also the clatter of dishes. Where was Blair? Not in his surgery at his house in Glencross, nor in his office in the gynaecological ward of the hospital, judging by the sounds she could hear.

'A relative of mine,' he replied at last. 'Look, Helen, I've got to go—I'm very busy this morning. I'll see you later, this evening at Castle Carroch.'

'When? What time? Just a minute——' she said urgently, but he had hung up.

She put down the receiver and stood for a moment frowning at the phone. She had wanted to ask him if he had a cold, because his voice had sounded different in some ways. It hadn't always sounded like his.

She laughed and shook her head, shaking away doubts and suspicions. Of course it had been Dr Blair Calder speaking to her. Only Blair would know he had invited her to go away with him for the weekend. She glanced at her watch. Another hour of work today, Friday, and then she could leave at noon to begin the long weekend holiday which was due to her. Returning to the laboratory, she sat down at the bench where she had been testing blood samples for their sugar content.

She was going away with Blair to spend two whole nights and nearly two days with him. She had committed herself at last to spending some time alone with the man who had been attracted to her ever since he had met her when she had first come to Glencross hospital to work as a lab technician nine months ago.

After that first meeting last September they had

become friends quite rapidly, although he had done all the pursuing, but because he was still married most of their meetings had been clandestine—to protect both their reputations, Blair had said, and because he was sueing his wife for a divorce and didn't want to give her a reason for sueing him. Helen had been disappointed when she had found out he was married and had tried to back away from having any sort of friendship with him, but he had persisted in seeing her.

To become emotionally and physically involved with another woman's husband had initially offended Helen's innate puritanism as well as her secret romantic attitude to life. She had always hoped, when she had thought of falling in love and getting married, that it would be with a man who was as free from commitment to another person as she was herself, and that she would be the first with him as he would be with her. She hadn't reckoned on being pursued by someone like Blair, who had managed to overcome her objections to going out with him occasionally when he had told her about the emptiness of his marriage to Wanda Murray, a well-known singing and recording star.

'Heaven knows why I ever married Wanda,' he had confided to Helen one day last October when they had driven out to Loch Lomond to walk beside the famous loch, which had been smooth and placid that autumn afternoon, reflecting not only the blue of the sky but also the bronze and yellow of dying leaves. 'I must have been out of my mind. But then I was young and impressionable and in those days she was ... well, she hadn't been hardened by success. She was only just beginning to be recorded. She started with a rock-n'-roll group, you know.'

'Yes, I have read about her,' Helen had replied. 'Where did you meet her?'

'Here in Glencross, as a matter of fact. She was at a party given for a friend of mine. The group Wanda was singing with played music for the dancing at the party.' He had sighed heavily. 'Yes, I was a fool in those days, believing that I had to marry a woman before I could have her. We were together only two years and then she walked out on me, said she couldn't get on with her career as a singer living here, that she had to go and live in London to be near the agents and recording studios. I'd just qualified as a gynaecologist and hoped to be appointed to a hospital in Glasgow, so I couldn't go with her. And that's when the splitting up began. For years we've lived apart, she in her apartment in London and me in the house up here.'

'Don't you ever meet?' Helen had exclaimed.

'Sometimes,' he had admitted. 'But it's ceased to be a proper marriage. She never does for me what a wife should do. She always puts herself and her career first.'

'Well, don't you put yourself and your career first?' Helen had challenged. 'Most men do, so I've heard.'

Blair had ignored her question and had continued to ramble on about how badly he felt Wanda had treated him.

'But one day soon, she'll give in and let me divorce her and then I'll be free again.' He had turned to her and had looked at her intently. 'I'll be free, then, to marry someone else,' he had added pointedly, 'someone less selfish, someone who will be a real wife. Someone like you, Helen.'

She hadn't risen to the bait—but then she hadn't refused to meet him and go out with him whenever

he had asked her either, and every time they had
met he had assured her that the time when Wanda
would agree to let him divorce her was coming
closer and closer.

'But it's getting harder and harder for me to
wait for you, Helen,' had been his refrain every
time he saw her, and his lovemaking had become
steadily more and more demanding.

'I want you, Helen,' he had whispered to her
only last Monday evening after kissing her rather
violently as they had said goodnight in his car
before she had gone up to her flat, and he had
gone on to suggest that he stay the night with her.
Somehow she had managed to persuade him that
it wouldn't be to his advantage if he were seen
leaving her flat the next morning and that if it
were discovered he had been with her all night
Wanda would have a good weapon to use against
him in a divorce case.

'You're right, absolutely right,' he had agreed,
much to her relief. 'But it makes no difference to
the way I feel about you. There must be something
we can do about it, somewhere we can go to be
really alone together. When do you have a long
weekend off?'

'This coming weekend.'

'I think I could manage to take some time off
then, too,' he had said. 'We could go somewhere
where no one will know us. I know just the place,
and it won't be too busy this time of the year.
When can you get away?'

'I finish at noon on Friday.'

'Good. I'll phone you later in the week to make
the final arrangements. Say you'll come away with
me, Helen. Please say it's what you want to do,'
he had pleaded, taking hold of her hands.

She had hesitated, feeling that she had been pulled in two different directions at once. Part of her, the sensible well-brought-up young woman, had insisted that she should refuse his invitation and that to go away and stay with him in an isolated place was to court disaster for herself. Blair would overwhelm her with his lovemaking and she would become just another woman who had succumbed in a moment of weakness to seduction by a married man. She would break her own code of honour and offend her own deep-rooted sense of good morality.

But the other part, the warm, sensitive, extremely feminine woman who was longing to fall in love and be swept off her feet by a passionate lover, had urged her to accept his invitation, seeing the weekend holiday with him as an adventure in romance, something that might never come her way again, if she refused. So ignoring the warning put out by her conscience, she had given in to his pleading and had agreed to go away with him for the weekend if he could make arrangements.

She left the hospital promptly at noon and drove in her small car—a secondhand one which her father had helped her to buy so that she could drive to her parents' home in Dumfries whenever she had the weekend off and wouldn't be dependent on buses or trains—to her flat in the nearby seaside town of Seakirk. She hadn't told her parents that she had this weekend off because she knew they would expect to see her in Dumfries. They knew nothing about Blair yet, because she had decided not to tell them about him until he was divorced from Wanda and was free to marry again. Then she might take him to meet them. Only *might*, she thought now with a rueful smile. They wouldn't approve of her going about with him while he was still married, and they would probably have reservations about her marrying a man who was divorced too. For them marriage between two people lasted until death, and they had no time for the permissive behaviour of the present younger generation.

She heated a small can of soup for her midday meal and, after eating, packed the clothes she would need for the weekend in a suitcase. At just after one, dressed in dark green pants, a crisp cotton tartan-printed blouse and a grey tweed jacket, she drove away from Seakirk, which was on the wide estuary of the Firth of Clyde, and drove north, through Gourock and Greenock to Erskine, where she crossed the River Clyde to Dunbartonshire.

Although the morning had been clear and sunny the weather had changed quickly as it often does on the west coast of Scotland. Thin grey nimbus clouds had spread across the sky and the river was a slightly darker grey, and as she drove onwards, northwards and then westwards into the mountains of Argyllshire, through narrow passes and then along the shore of the wide sea loch of Loch Fyne, the clouds grew heavier, hiding the summits of the mountains.

Three and a half hours after leaving her flat she turned off the road to Oban from Lochgilphead on to a country road which wound past lush green meadows where brown cattled grazed, on her way at last to Ballacuish. She came upon the village abruptly around a bend in the road. It was only a line of whitewashed cottages strung out beside the road, each one with its patch of garden. Then she was past them and the road was merely a gravel track which ended rather suddenly at the front door of a squat single-storey cottage built of stone and set at right angles to the sea.

There was a small van parked by the cottage, so Helen parked her car beside it, took out her case and locked the car's doors. Looking round, she noticed the jetty and began to walk towards it. In the shelter of the sturdy stone walls built in the shape of an ell, which jutted out into the water, a small black motorboat was tied up. Across the narrow strait of water lay several islands, some small and green, some more mountainous, dark blue shapes crowned with misty grey clouds.

'You wouldn't be Miss Melrose now, would you? Miss Helen Melrose?' asked a masculine voice behind her; a deep voice speaking with the cadence of the born Highlander. Helen spun round in surprise, the hairs pricking on the back of her neck. She hadn't heard him walk up behind her.

'Oh, you gave me an awful fright!' she gasped. 'Are you Mr Magnus?'

'Just Magnus,' he replied. 'There's no need for you to be calling me Mister. You are Helen Melrose, then?'

'Yes, I am.'

'You are not at all what I was expecting,' he remarked frankly, his glance roving over her. 'I thought you would be older.'

'You're not what I was expecting either,' she retorted, her chin going up at a defiant angle. She didn't like the way his vivid blue eyes were appraising her. 'I thought you'd be older too.'

His dark level eyebrows lifted slightly and a slight smile quirked his long lips, but he made no further comment. He wasn't as old as Blair, she decided, possibly in his early thirties, and he was

tall and lean, dressed in navy blue corduroy pants
tucked into rubber sea-boots and a plain navy-blue
jersey with a crew-neck, which left his strong,
suntanned neck exposed. Over the jersey he wore a
bright yellow waterproof jacket, the sort often
worn by sailors of yachts in bad weather. Its collar
was turned up, forming a frame for his long-jawed,
rather gaunt face. Dark brown hair coiled about
his forehead and ears in wind-blown dishevelment.
There was about him a reckless, free-booting
appearance. He wasn't at all her idea of a
caretaker, not at all staid and solid, slow-moving
and slow-thinking but dependable. No, not at all
dependable-looking.

They both became aware that they were staring
at each other in a curiously tense silence because
they both looked away from each other and spoke
at the same time.

'Dr Calder said you would take me over to the
island,' Helen said.

'Give me your case and I'll put it in the boat,'
said Magnus.

Helen turned and looked at him again, suspicion
clouding her mind. Now she wasn't at all sure she
should go with this ruffian.

'Perhaps I'd better wait for Dr Calder,' she said.
'And then we can all cross to the island together.
It seems pointless for you to take me over and
then have to come back again for him.'

The blue eyes—they were that clear Celtic blue
found so often in the people who inhabit the
islands and Highlands of Scotland, the blue of
harebells which grow wild on the sprawling tawny
moors—narrowed thoughtfully and a frown pulled
his eyebrows together across the bridge of his long
nose.

'It would be a long wait, I'm thinking,' he said at last. 'And when I was talking on the phone with Dr Calder. . . .'

'When? When were you talking to him?' Helen asked quickly.

'This morning,' he replied coolly. 'He told me he wouldn't be arriving until about eight o'clock this evening but that you would be coming this afternoon, and he asked me to take you over to the island straight away, so I think we should do as he suggested.'

He picked up her case and dropped it into the motorboat which he had pulled in close to the jetty, and with a graceful gesture of one lean hand he indicated that she should go down the few stone steps which were showing above the lapping water and get into the boat. Still suspicious of him because he didn't fit in with her preconception of what a caretaker should be like, Helen hesitated, giving him another wary glance. He looked back at her steadily, his eyes blank, his mouth set in a straight unsmiling line.

'Are you sure you won't mind doing two trips?' she asked, unable to find any other reason for not going with him.

'I'm sure. Do not be worrying about it, but think of it from my point of view. If I am not obeying Dr Calder's instructions and taking you over to the island he will be annoyed and I might lose my job. And jobs are hard to come by in this part of the country for the likes of me.'

'Yes, I suppose they are,' she agreed. 'All right, I'll go with you.'

She stepped into the boat and sat down in one of the padded seats. Magnus untied the rope which had held the boat to the jetty, stepped aboard and started the engine immediately as the boat began to drift away from the jetty. While they had been talking a faint breeze, coming from the south-west, had begun to blow. It ruffled the water and seagulls soared on the currents of air, flashes of white against the darkening grey of sky and sea.

Putting the engine in gear, Magnus turned the steering wheel, pointed the bow of the boat towards the island and opened the throttle. Over the swirling water the boat surged, flinging up white spray. Speech was impossible because of the roar of the motor, and anyway, Helen couldn't think of anything to say to her rather wild impassive companion, and he didn't seem to be at all interested in conversing with her now that he had got her in the boat. The distance to Carroch was much farther than she had imagined it would be, and it wasn't until the cottage on the mainland shore and the jetty below it were merely grey blurred shapes seen through thick grey air brought by the south-westerly wind that she was able to see the reddish cliffs of Carroch and an opening in them of a small bay rimmed with sand.

A jetty similar to the one they had left jutted out into the bay and Magnus guided the boat behind its protective wall, stopped the engine and sprang ashore, the rope in his hand. Helen lifted her case up to him, then climbed out of the boat, noticing as she did the clarity of the water. Rocks and mud shone up from the bottom and blue mussel-shells glinted. A shoal of tiny greyish-green iridescent fish flitted by.

'The castle is at the southern end of the island, looking down the Sound towards the hills and Kintyre and the mountains of the island of Jura,' said Magnus. 'You will not be minding the walk?'

'No. I like walking.'

'Some parts of the path are a wee bit boggy, but if you follow where I lead you'll avoid them,' he added, and lifting her case to one shoulder he set off up a narrow path which passed into the grey gloom of closely planted pine trees, protected from wind and salt spray on this sheltered eastern side of the island. The path was matted with many layers of the tiny brown pine needles and the feathery branches of the trees swayed and sighed in the wind. As she followed Magnus through the scented gloom of the little wood Helen felt she had been whisked away from the noise and cares of modern life to a magic place where it was possible to believe the 'wee folk' of Celtic mythology, the kelpies and the fairies, lived.

Emerging from the wood at a higher level than they had entered it, they had to brace themselves against the increased force of the wind as it swept across an expanse of tufted green and tawny moorland, scattered with outcrops of rock and starred with wild flowers. The fronds of bracken were thick and strong and where a small stream trickled the straight swordlike leaves of wild irises clustered.

They came to the castle suddenly, dropping down from the crown of the moor by a narrow twisting path to a door in a stone wall that protected a garden laid out behind the square stone tower. Magnus opened the door and went through first, holding it open for her, and then they walked across the garden, following a neat pathway between rows and rows of vegetable seedlings which Helen recognised as carrots, peas, potatoes and beans, from an intimate knowledge of her father's garden in Dumfries.

'Your garden is looking very well,' she said falling into step beside Magnus as they approached the addition to the plain square tower, a smaller building two storeys high which had a sloping slate roof.

'The garden?' he repeated, giving her a puzzled frowning look and then glancing beyond her at the neat rows. 'Ach yes, it's coming along fine, just fine,' he added quickly, then strode forward, leaving her to follow him again, and she had the distinct impression that he had no interest whatever in gardening and that the row of vegetables had not been planted by him.

They entered the additional wing of the castle through a porch where Magnus took off his sea-boots and hung up his yellow jacket. Opening another door, he led the way into the big kitchen which seemed to have all the necessary modern equipment, a gleaming gas cooker, stainless steel sinks, formica working surfaces, cupboards and a refrigerator, as well as a scrubbed deal table and a dresser, its shelves filled with old willow pattern plates. There was a wide stone fireplace too, its dog grate filled with paper and kindling ready for lighting, should a fire be needed.

Beside the fireplace another doorway led straight into the ground floor of the tower, which had been divided into a narrow hallway of which doors opened into two rooms one on either side. A narrow stone staircase slanted up from the hallway following one of the thick walls of the tower to a second-floor landing. Helen followed Magnus up the stairs and he led her into a wide room with a single latticed window.

'The view from the window is that of the Sound and is magnificent on a good day,' he said, putting down her case. 'But you won't be seeing much today. I'm thinking we're in for a storm tonight.'

'I hope it doesn't get too stormy,' said Helen anxiously, glancing out of the window at the shoreline below the castle and the grey waves hurling themselves against reefs of jagged rocks. Beyond the waves there was nothing, only greenish-grey murk covering everything, blotting out views of islands and mountains. She glanced at her watch. It was almost five-thirty. 'I hope you'll be able to get across to fetch Dr Calder,' she added.

'I'll leave you now to unpack,' Magnus replied coolly, turning his back on her and going towards the door. 'If you want anything to eat or to drink just help yourself in the kitchen.'

'Oh, don't you live in the castle?' she asked, going after him. In spite of the pleasant comfort of the room, the rose-patterned curtains and bed-cover, the pink carpet, the simple pinewood furniture, she felt she didn't want to be left alone. On that fast darkening afternoon the old castle had an eerie atmosphere. Magnus looked back at her from the doorway and the cold blankness of his eyes, the hard gauntness of his face, did nothing to reassure her.

'Yes, I live in it,' he replied.

'And your wife lives here too?'

'I don't have a wife.'

'Then who keeps house?'

'What do you mean?'

'I thought ... I assumed there must be a housekeeper to cook and clean for the owner. Dr Calder told me that the place is owned by a relative of his.'

'That's right, but there is no housekeeper. Mrs

Macleish comes over once a week to clean the place and Archie, her husband, looks after the garden. They live at the croft by the jetty on the mainland, where you left your car,' he said, and left the room.

He wasn't exactly friendly thought Helen, as she lifted her suitcase to a low blanket chest which was situated below the window. She clicked undone the locks and began to take out clothes and hang them in the wardrobe, puzzling over the enigma of Magnus. There was something vaguely familiar about him. She felt she had seen him before. But then maybe he was just typical of the people who live in the Highlands and Islands of Scotland and that was why he seemed familiar.

When she had finished unpacking she left the bedroom and went downstairs to the hallway, pausing there to listen. All she could hear was the whining of the wind and the crash of the waves on the shore. No lights were on in the hallway or in the rooms off it. The tower was silent and dark. Not liking the feeling of being alone that was creeping over her, Helen went quickly into the kitchen hoping to find Magnus there, but the room was empty and dim.

Quickly she snapped on the light switch, thankful that the castle had electricity, and went across to the window to pull across the bright chintz curtains and shut out the wild storm-grey light of late afternoon. Searching through the cupboards, she found a tea-pot, tea-cups, and saucers. In the fridge there was plenty of milk and other foods, lamb chops, a roast of beef, frozen vegetables, butter and eggs. Presumably Mrs Macleish had stocked up when she had been informed that Dr Calder would be staying at the castle for the weekend.

She made a pot of tea and found a tin of biscuits, turned on the transistor radio and sat for a while at the table drinking tea and nibbling and listening to the usual programme of music transmitted before the news. When the news came on she turned the radio off, not wanting to listen to the usual headlines about the economic recession, wars and strikes, and parliamentary argument. Soon Blair would be arriving at the Macleishes' croft. Had Magnus gone to meet him? Was that where he had gone? She hoped so.

Should she start preparing a meal for herself and Blair? Or should she wait until he arrived? She decided to wait. It would be fun to prepare a meal together in this well-equipped kitchen and then eat it in another room. On sudden impulse she left the kitchen and went into the tower, switching on the hall light. She stepped into the room directly opposite the kitchen and turned on the light in there. It was a dining room furnished with a long antique Jacobean refectory table, a beautiful piece, its surface highly polished. On either side of the table were the customary long oak benches and at either end there were high-backed intricately carved Jacobean chairs. To Helen's way of thinking the room looked ready to receive guests dressed in seventeenth-century clothes. The ladies would be in low-cut full-skirted gowns and the men in satin breeches, silk stockings and long-skirted coats, and would carry plumed hats.

Leaving the formality of the dining room, Helen crossed the hallway and went into the other room. To her surprise it was much more modern and casual in its furnishing, with two big upholstered sofas covered with chintz slip-on covers, occasional tables and several armchairs. Under the window there was a big desk on which there was a typewriter. Papers were heaped beside the machine and opened books were scattered across the desk. Books filled the shelves on either side of the wide stone fireplace too and on one of the occasional tables close to a sofa there was a decanter of what looked like whisky and an empty glass. The room looked as if someone had been in it recently and had just got up and walked out. Who? Magnus?

Surely not. A caretaker would hardly make himself at home in his employer's living room, would he? More likely Blair's relative had been here the previous weekend and had left this room in the state it was. But then if Mrs Macleish had been over to clean wouldn't she have taken the empty glass away to wash it and put the decanter away where it belonged? And wouldn't whoever had used the typewriter have removed the typed page which was still inserted into it, collected up all the other typewritten pages and put them away in a folder, closed the books and perhaps returned them to the shelves?

Wind buffeted the window which faced the shore and Helen looked up from reading the words on the sheet of paper which was in the typewriter—it seemed to be some sort of script, possibly for a play—and glanced out of the window. Sullen almost black clouds were rolling across the sky now and the sea was churned up by the wind into white-crested waves. What was it like in the strait between Carroch and the other island? Had Magnus been able to cross over in the motorboat? And if he had managed to get across would it be possible for him and Blair to come to

Carroch? She hoped so, she sincerely hoped so, because she didn't fancy spending the night alone in this wild isolated place.

Suddenly her skin prickled. She felt she was being watched. Whirling round, she looked around the room and then at the open door. There was no one in the room nor standing at the doorway. Quickly she walked over to the doorway and looked out into the hallway. No one there either. The stairway creaked and she looked up it. Was someone moving in the shadows up there? She found another light switch and flicked it. Light came on on the second landing. Slowly Helen mounted the stairs. There was no one on the landing, but it seemed to her that the flight of stairs leading up to the third storey also creaked, and she looked up them, trying to probe the black shadows.

The wind whined and her courage deserted her all at once. Turning, she ran into her bedroom, flicking on the light, took her raincoat from the wardrobe and pulled it on. Without switching off the light she ran from the room and down the stairs, tying a scarf around her head as she went. Right through the kitchen she ran and into the porch, wrenching the door open and rushing out into the windy evening. She slammed the door behind her and walked quickly through the garden. Soon she was climbing the path to the moor. Behind her the lights she had left on in the castle twinkled through the grey mist brought by the south-west wind. Slowly, although Helen did not see because she was too busy hurrying across the moor, blown by the wind, the lights went out, starting with the one in her bedroom, then the landing light, the living room light and the dining room light, the hallway light, until only the kitchen light was on.

The pinewood was darker than ever, but she found her way along the path, sometimes sliding on the slippery pine needles in her haste to reach the little bay and the jetty. She was driven by a strange fear of the unknown, of the castle and its caretaker and by a need to see another human being.

As soon as she saw the strait her heart sank. No boat as small as the motorboat in which Magnus had brought her to the island could possibly make the crossing in such wild conditions. The water, not as tossed as the sea was on the other side of the island admittedly, was swirling by in a series of whirlpools, seething and hissing, perpetually boiling, and visibility was so bad she couldn't see anything of the opposite shore, not even a twinkle of light in the Macleish cottage. Yet there was no boat bobbing about and pulling at its mooring line in the small harbour made by the jetty walls, so Magnus must have set out.

Helen wasn't sure how long she stood at the end of the jetty trying to pierce the increasing gloom, trying to see if there was a small black boat leaping over the boiling water on its way back to Carroch, but after a while she became aware that she was shivering and that she had seen nothing. She glanced at her watch. It was well after seven and getting darker every minute, although on a normal evening at this time of the year the sun would not have set yet.

But this was not a normal evening and it looked very much as if she was going to spend the night alone at the castle. How she wished she had stayed on the other side of the strait and had waited for

Blair to come! If she had she would be with him
now and perhaps they would have been driving to
Oban to have dinner in a hotel and perhaps to stay
the night there, instead of being separated like this
by wind and weather.

Reluctantly she turned and began to trudge up
the path to the wood. It would be best if she
returned to the castle while there was still some
light or she might get lost on the moor. From the
shelter of the pinewood she battled out against the
wind, pushing against it with all her might,
occasionally plunging into a boggy bit of turf,
filling her shoes with mud and slime. At last she
reached the edge of the moor and saw the light in
the kitchen window of the castle wing. Strange
that no other lights were showing. She was sure
she hadn't turned them off.

Her shoes squelching as she walked she made
her way through the garden to the back porch,
opened the door and stepped inside. From the
kitchen, through the door which was still closed,
came the sound of music; bagpipe music. Helen's
skin chilled. Who was in there? What would she
see when she opened the door? The wee folk
dancing to the sound of the pipes?

Gritting her teeth, she took hold of the latch
and lifted it and pushed the door open. She
stepped inside and closed the door after her, then
looked round, half-fearfully, and gasped with
amazement. Sitting at the table eating, his dark
ruffled hair glinting with golden lights under the
glow of the electric light, was Magnus. The
bagpipe music was coming from the transistor
radio.

He looked up and across at her and it seemed
to her that his blue eyes danced with secret

amusement, although it might have only been the glitter of the light in them.

'But how did you get here without me seeing you come back from the jetty?' she exclaimed, staring at him.

He switched off the radio which was on the table before answering her.

'I haven't been to the jetty,' he replied coolly, continuing to eat. He was having lamb chops, potato chips and peas, and the smell of cooking still lingered on the air, making Helen realise how hungry she was.

'You mean you were here in the house when I went out?' she said, advancing slowly towards the table, remembering how the stairs had creaked and her suspicions that someone had been watching her.

'I was.' A faint smile twitched at his lips and again the blue eyes seemed to glint with wicked amusement. 'I put out the lights you left on,' he added dryly.

'Then ... Then you didn't go in the boat to meet Blair.'

'No, I did not go in the boat to meet Blair,' he said, unkindly mimicking her Lowland accent, and she realised suddenly that he had been speaking to her without any accent at all and without any of the Gaelic phrasing he had used when speaking to her earlier. He had changed. He was no longer a vague, somewhat wild islander glad to have the job of looking after a castle for its owner. He was a calm, confident, sophisticated person, fully in control of the situation and more than a little amused by her bewilderment. 'You see, Blair isn't coming here,' he added.

'Not coming? Has he phoned you again?' Helen

untied the knot in her headscarf and drew it off
her head. Her blonde hair shimmered silkily in the
electric light as she shook it free. It had come loose
from its confining clasp and flowed freely about
her face and shoulders.

'No, he hasn't,' Magnus replied.

'Then how do you know he isn't coming?'

'I know because he didn't plan to come here at
all,' he said calmly, and finished eating the food on
his plate.

'But he phoned me this morning to tell me we
were coming here. And he phoned you too,' she
said in puzzlement, her suspicions sharpening as
she stared at him. 'Did he tell you he wasn't
coming here when he phoned you earlier?' she
demanded. 'Oh, if he did, you should have told me
and I'd have gone back to Glencross. I wouldn't
have come here with you. Oh, why didn't you give
me his message? Why didn't you tell me?'

'Because I wanted you to come here with me,'
he replied softly. 'I wanted to separate you from
Blair and prevent you from spending the weekend
with him.'

Her tawny brown eyes wide in her suddenly very
pale face, Helen took hold of the back of one of
the spindle-backed chairs and pulled it out from
the table. She sank down on it as if her legs had
turned to jelly. She felt as if she had been caught in
one of those strange dreams in which there was no
logic, and across the table she stared at the man
who called himself Magnus but who was no longer
the Magnus who had brought her across to the
island, hearing again the cadence of the voice
which had spoken to her over the phone that
morning, the slight difference there had been in it
from Blair's voice; a difference she hadn't been

able to describe when she had first heard it but which she now recognised as a deep resonance which Blair's voice didn't have but this man's did have.

'It was you, this morning, on the phone,' she whispered. 'You pretended you were Blair!'

'I did.' He grinned suddenly, teeth flashing white; a mischievous mocking grin which robbed his lean face of its austereness and gave it a boyish warmth. 'And I must have done a pretty good job of imitating him too, because you fell for it; you agreed to come here, and now you're going to stay with me for the whole weekend, until Monday afternoon, just as you would have stayed with him.'

'No, I'm not. I'm not staying here with you!' retorted Helen. 'You can't make me stay here with you!' She sprang to her feet, hoping to break the dream, hoping to find herself in bed at her flat on the mainland; hoping to find that Friday morning was only just dawning and that she hadn't yet agreed to meet Blair and go away with him for the weekend. But the dream didn't break. She was still there in the castle's kitchen and the man called Magnus was leaning back on his chair, tipping it on to its back legs, *keckling*, her mother would have called it, and doing the chair legs no good at all. And he was still grinning at her mockingly.

'I'm not staying here any longer,' she insisted loudly. 'I'm leaving now.' She turned about and made for the porch, charging towards it rather blindly. Surely when she opened the door and left the kitchen the dream would end.

But he was there before her, long and lean and somehow devilish, blocking her way. Again she turned and stared across the room towards the hallway, intending to leave by the front door, only to collide with him when he stepped in front of her again. Hands on her shoulders, he held her upright when she lost her balance.

'Let me go! Take your hands off me!' she seethed.

'Not until you stop behaving like a fool,' he said sternly, giving her a shake. 'Where would you go on this island if you don't stay here? It's getting stormier by the minute outside and there's no other shelter on the island. None at all. Unless you fancy spending the night in the old boathouse. But I wouldn't recommend it—it's very damp.'

'The boat!' she exclaimed. 'Where is it? It wasn't at the jetty, so I thought you must have gone over for Blair in it. Oh, it must have broken loose and been washed away.'

'In that case,' he drawled softly, his eyes seeming to soften and darken, his hand moving gently and caressingly along her shoulders, fingers sliding amongst the silkiness of her hair, 'we are well and truly stranded here, together, but not to worry— we have plenty of food and drink. And we have each other for company. No need for either of us to feel lonely, Eilidh.' His voice deepened. 'No need at all.'

Mesmerised by the sensuous expression in his eyes, by the musical seduction of his voice, Jelen made no attempt to move or to break free of his hold, even though she knew that she should if she wanted to avoid being kissed by him. As if in a trance she watched his face come closer. It blurred. She saw one intensely blue eye fringed with black lashes, felt the tip of his nose and the roughness of his jaw against her cheek and then his lips were pressing against hers and she was being kissed as she had never been kissed before, not even by Blair, slowly and expertly, until her head was whirling and she had to close her eyes against a sudden dizziness of desire.

CHAPTER TWO

What am I doing? Why am I letting this stranger kiss me like this? The cool sensible part of Helen suddenly asserted itself, overcoming the inner passionate woman who was longing to be loved, and she pushed free of Magnus's hold and wrenched her lips from his. For a moment of tense silence they stood still close to each other staring, she glaring at him in outrage, on the verge of slapping his face, he frowning at her in puzzlement. Then as if to underline what he had said about the storminess of the weather the wind howled in the chimney and the window rattled, drawing the attention of both of them to it.

'You see how foolish and impractical it would be for you to go out now?' Magnus said smoothly. 'Why don't you take your coat off and sit down,' he continued, turning away from her and going over to the cooker. 'In anticipation of your return I cooked enough chops for two and it won't take me long to fry up some more chips. I'm sure you must be hungry.'

Slightly disconcerted by the quick change in him from would-be lover to practical cook, Helen stayed where she was, watching him out of the corners of her eyes. She could leave now, while his back was turned. She could run from the house through the back door. But where would she run to? Again the wind howled and the window rattled, and she shivered suddenly, imagining the

wildness outside, the black clouds racing across
the sky, the sea roaring and heaving. Out there
everything would be moving and uncertain and
dark and she could easily get lost. In here
everything was still and bright and the only danger
was the man who was now emptying sliced
potatoes from a colander into a pan of smoking
hot fat. The fat spat and sizzled when the cold,
damp potatoes hit it.

Slowly, admitting reluctantly that he was right
and it would be foolish and impractical for her to
go out into the storm, Helen slipped off her
raincoat and, after putting it over the back of one
chair, she sat down in another.

'Why? Why did you pretend to be Blair and
suggest that I came here?' she demanded.

Magnus glanced at her over one shoulder,
his bright blue glance flashing vividly like light-
ning before he looked back at the cooking
chips.

'To help a friend of mine,' he replied laconically,
giving the pan a shake to move the chips around in
the fat. 'Knives and forks are in the right-hand
drawer of the dresser if you'd like to get them for
yourself. I don't mind cooking for you this time,
but I hope you don't expect me to wait upon you
hand and foot while you stay here,' he added
mockingly.

'I don't expect anything from you,' she retorted, getting to her feet and going over to the
dresser. 'I'm quite capable of looking after
myself.'

'Good. I'm glad to hear it, because looking after
people isn't my line at all.' He gave her another
bright sardonic glance. 'That's why I'm not
married. You won't catch me fetching and

carrying for a woman or slaving at a nine-to-five job just to provide her with a roof over her head and clothes to dress up in.'

'Oh, I have no difficulty in imagining that you're selfish to the core,' Helen scoffed as she set a place for herself on the table. 'And most women with any common sense would avoid a man like you like the plague. No woman worth her salt wants to be married to a selfish egotist.'

'Ha!' His laugh was short but truly amused. 'That's a sharp tongue you have, Eilidh Melrose.' He looked at her again, more slowly this time, his glance lingering deliberately on her lips, then on her softly rounded chin and then on the shapes of her breasts, taut under the poplin of her blouse, until she felt the blood rising willy-nilly to her cheeks and had to subdue a wild urge to pick something up from the table and throw it at him. His eyes met her wrathful glare and he grinned at her again, mockingly. 'Do you know that Blair is married to Wanda Murray?' he asked casually.

'Yes, I do. He told me,' she replied stiffly.

'And yet you were going away with him for the weekend, for two nights and two days, in fact. Tut, tut, Eilidh!' he clocked his tongue tauntingly. 'What would your friends and relatives say if they knew you're having a torrid love affair with a married man?'

'Blair and I are not having a ... a torrid affair!' she retorted furiously. 'We ... well, we're just good friends. Anyway, his marriage is a farce. He and Wanda hardly ever see each other now.'

'Don't they?' he queried dryly. 'Are you sure?'

'Blair told me they've been separated for nearly five years.'

'And you believed him, of course,' he remarked with heavy irony as he took a plate out of the oven on which there were two lamb chops and began to scoop up chips from the pan to put on the plate. 'He can make up quite a good story when he wants to,' he continued, coming across to the table and setting the plate of food down in front of her. 'And when he wants something,' he added dryly. 'Something he can't have. Presumably he wanted you, but you wouldn't play, so he told you the sad tale of his marriage to Wanda and you felt sorry for him and agreed to go away with him this weekend.'

'You know nothing about Blair and me,' she defended hotly. 'Nothing at all. And you have no right to sneer at us!'

'I know enough,' he retorted, sitting down in the chair opposite to her. 'And I know Wanda. It was to help her that I pretended to be Blair and invited you to come here today. You see, she wanted to see him this weekend. She wanted to have him to herself.' He glanced at his wristwatch. 'She and Blair must have met by now and they could be on their way to the place he had planned to take you.'

Helen looked down at the plate in front of her. The lamb chops were small but looked succulent. The chips were crisp and golden. Her mouth watered, and picking up her knife and fork she began to cut into one of the chops.

'I don't understand how Blair's wife could possibly know about me or that he and I had planned to go away together this weekend,' she said after a while. 'We've tried to be careful.'

'*You* may have been careful, but Blair hasn't. He likes to boast of his amorous conquests, particularly to Wanda. It's his way of drawing her attention to him. He'd told her he had a new girl-friend, so all she had to do was to have him watched.'

'Watched?' exclaimed Helen. 'What do you mean? Have you been watching him?'

'Good grief, no. I've much better things to do with my time than to spend it spying on Blair,' he replied disgustedly.

'Then who has been watching him?'

'A private detective employed by an agency that searches for missing persons and keeps tabs on erring husbands. Or wives.' His lips curled scornfully. 'It's not a job I'd like to do. I'm not keen on spies of any sort.'

'You just prefer to do the kidnapping, I suppose,' she remarked acidly.

'But I haven't kidnapped you,' he replied mildly. 'I merely invited you to come to Carroch and you came.'

'You deceived me by impersonating Blair and you've prevented me from leaving this island!' she hissed at him.

'I haven't prevented you from leaving. The weather has done that,' he retorted.

Helen was silent again as she went on eating, although it seemed to her that the food had lost its taste. Blair had told Wanda that he had a girl-friend! After agreeing to keep their meetings as secret as possible he had then betrayed her to his wife. Oh, how could he have done that to her? How could he? And he had been watched. For how long? For how many weeks or months had his goings and comings to and from the hospital, to and from his house, to and from her small flat, been watched by observant suspicious eyes?

And if he had been watched he had been seen with her, and that meant her goings and comings had been subsequently watched too. Oh, it made her feel sick to think of being spied upon! It made her flesh creep to think of some obscure little man—he had to be little so that no one noticed him, she argued—wearing a raincoat and a tweed cap so as to be inconspicuous, watching Blair and herself. It made her feel cheap, and that had the effect of spoiling her friendship with Blair and all her outings with him. It made her feel she never wanted to see him again. Never.

'Eat up,' said Magnus, his voice deep and soft. 'No point in going hungry just because you're angry.'

She looked across at him. He was keckling the chair again, leaning back with his hands in his pants pockets, and he was watching her, his lean face devoid of expression, and now he seemed like no one she had ever met before; not like the wild islander who had met her at Macleish's cottage; not like the cool sophisticate who had welcomed her when she had returned to the kitchen; and not at all like the sensualist who had kissed her as she had never been kissed before. He seemed to have the ability to change his personality quickly, like a chameleon changes its appearance, and now he seemed like a friend, someone who was concerned about her welfare.

'Wouldn't you be angry if you'd just realised you'd been spied on for weeks, possibly for months?'

'I suppose I would,' he admitted. 'But who are you angry with?'

'With you, for imitating Blair and deceiving me into coming here. And with Wanda for paying someone to spy on Blair and me.'

'But not with Blair or yourself?' he jibed, changing again from a friend into a foe, bewildering her. 'You know, if you hadn't decided to have an affair with Blair in the first place Wanda wouldn't have had to pay someone to spy on him or on you, and I wouldn't have had to imitate Blair so as to entice you to come here.'

'I've told you already,' said Helen, speaking slowly and clearly as if to a deaf person, 'Blair and I have not been having an affair; not in the way you mean.'

'Oh, sorry—I forgot,' he jeered sarcastically. 'You're just good friends, aren't you? You'll be telling me next that he's never talked about getting married to you as soon as he's managed to divorce Wanda.'

Helen had no retort to make to that. She could only look at him, the expression on her fair face betraying that Blair had talked about marriage to her.

'He says it to all his girl-friends,' Magnus went on as if she had admitted openly to him that Blair had suggested marriage. 'So never think you're the first.' His glance was pitying. 'There was the woman doctor in a hospital in Glasgow, a nurse somewhere else, a model in Paris, the American student he met when on holiday in Greece. . . .'

'Oh, stop it, stop it!' Helen cried. 'I don't want to hear any more of your lies!'

'Or you don't want to hear there've been others before you,' he scoffed. 'If it's any comfort to you, you've lasted the longest, and now that I've met you I think I can understand why.'

'I don't believe Blair is like you say he is,' she retorted. 'Anyway, if he's had so many extra-marital relationships why hasn't Wanda divorced him?'

'That's exactly what I . . . and her other friends . . . have been asking for some time,' he said, and gave her a vividly blue ironic glance. 'Maybe she's been blinded by love to his faults, like you are,' he suggested mockingly, and stood up. 'You might wash up when you've finished eating.'

He strode from the room and she heard his footsteps retreating up the stairs. Left alone, she sat at the table for a while poking with her fork at the cold food left on her plate, thinking over what Magnus had told her. *Blinded by love.* His scornful remark cut to the quick. Was it true? Was he right? Had growing affection for Blair blinded her so that he had been able to lead her on these past nine months, lead her into this present dangerous situation?

Picking up her plate, she carried it over to the sink, emptied the uneaten food into the garbage bin and automatically turned on the taps to fill the sink with water for washing up. By the time she had washed and dried the few dishes and had cleaned the pans she had decided that it was important to get in touch with Blair. She would phone his house and if he was there she would tell him exactly what had happened. Poor man, he must be in a terrible state wondering where she was and why she hadn't been at her flat when he had called to pick her up.

On the other hand, if he wasn't at home, if what Magnus had told her was true and Blair had gone off with his wife somewhere, she would try to find out from his housekeeper where he had gone and then try to contact him at that place. And she would ask him outright if he was with Wanda.

Hanging up the tea-towel she had been using, she left the kitchen to go in search of a telephone. There wasn't one in the hallway on the small antique table and she couldn't recall having seen one in the dining room. Where might there be one? On the desk in the lounge, she suspected. Crossing the hallway, she pushed open the lounge door. Two lamps were on, the table lamp on the desk and a standard lamp behind one of the big armchairs. Magnus was sitting in the chair, his feet resting on a small footstool. He was reading what seemed to be a thick sheaf of papers. Beside him on an oval rosewood occasional table was the decanter of whisky and a glass half-full of liquor. Helen cleared her throat, but he didn't look at her.

'Is there a phone in the house?' she asked.

'No.' He went on reading.

She frowned, sure that he was lying. After all, he had phoned her this morning. Perhaps he had hidden it. She went over to the desk and began to move the books and papers which were scattered about.

'What are you doing?' he demanded sharply. 'Leave those things alone!'

'I thought the phone might be hidden under them,' she replied, turning to look at him. He hadn't changed his position, but he had lowered the sheaf of papers and was scowling at her.

'Didn't you hear me say no to your question?' he said.

'Yes, I did, but I didn't believe you. How could I? You tell lies all the time,' she returned coolly.

'Damn!' He grated the word out through thinning lips and his eyes blazed blue murder at her. 'There isn't a phone in this house,' he enunciated very coldly and clearly, and picking up the glass he drank all the whisky that was in it.

'Then where did you phone from this morning?' Helen challenged, advancing towards him.

'From the Macleishes' kitchen,' he replied, and picking up the decanter poured a generous dram of whisky into the glass.

'Oh.' Feeling deflated because she was unable to phone Blair and speak to him or find out from his housekeeper where he had gone, Helen sat down on the edge of the sofa. Now she felt really stranded—in more ways than one. She felt absolutely cut off from reality, trapped in a nightmare with a strange man, whose character kept changing so that she couldn't be sure he was real at all. She glanced sideways at him. He was reading again, taking no notice of her at all, and that in itself was an affront.

'I wish I knew how you knew that Blair had invited me to go away with him this weekend,' she said with a sigh.

'Wanda told me,' he replied laconically, but didn't look at her.

'But how did she know? I didn't tell anyone. And I don't think Blair did either.'

Magnus raised his head, pushing back dishevelled hair from his forehead, and looked at her with a touch of exasperation.

'Of course you told someone. You told the secretary at the hospital lab you'd be off this weekend. And the personnel department would know you had a holiday due,' he said curtly.

'But I didn't tell anyone I was going away with Blair,' she insisted stubbornly.

'You didn't have to. Blair's receptionist and his housekeeper knew he was going away for three days too, and it wouldn't be hard for a good private enquiry agent to acquire such information about you and Blair and give it to Wanda. She put two and two together, basing her calculation on what she already knew about you and Blair. And you confirmed her suspicions when I phoned you this morning. What was it you said? *"Are we still going away for the weekend?"* '

He imitated her way of speaking again and picking up the glass drank more whisky. Over the rim of the glass his eyes met hers mockingly.

'I think you're hateful,' Helen muttered. 'You're a deceitful liar, pretending to be what you're not all the time!'

'I can't say I think very highly of you,' he retorted contemptuously. 'You meet another woman's husband on the sly and you plan to go away with him for two whole days and nights. I suppose you were hoping to seduce him, get pregnant by him so that he'd be forced to marry you. . . .'

'I haven't! I wasn't hoping to . . . to seduce him or get pregnant,' she gasped, her cheeks flushing scarlet again. 'Oh, I'm not like that at all.'

'No?' His eyebrows went up derisively and she

would have given anything to have been near enough to slap his face and wipe the mocking sneer from his shapely lips.

'It was Blair's idea that we should go away together,' she added lamely.

'It takes two to tango,' he jibed, setting down his empty glass. 'You could have refused to go away with him.'

About to open her mouth and make another angry retort, Helen subdued the impulse, wondering how she had managed to become involved in a slanging match with this irritating man. Why should it matter to her what he thought of her? He was, after all, only the caretaker of the castle—and a drunken one too, judging by the way he consumed quantities of neat whisky, she thought scathingly, flicking an underbrowed glance in his direction.

'You said this morning that this place is owned by a relative of Blair's,' she said.

'I did.'

'You said also that you're the caretaker. At least, when I asked you who Magnus was you said, "You could say he's the caretaker of the castle." '

'That's right. That's what I said.'

'Well, I can't imagine that the owner of the castle would be any too pleased with you if he walked in now and saw you loafing in this room, drinking his whisky,' she said acidly.

'The whisky is mine,' he replied coolly, returning her accusing stare with a cold one of his own. 'And I have permission from the owner to treat the castle just as if it's my home.' He tossed the sheaf of papers on to the floor, swung his legs down for the footstool and leaning forward, resting his folded arms on his knees, he stared at her more intently, the expression in his eyes changing, becoming warmer, kinder. 'Look, Eilidh,' he said softly, 'I realise you're hurt, upset by what you've found out about Blair this afternoon.'

'I still don't believe what you've said about him,' she said woodenly, looking away from him. 'And I won't believe it until I've spoken to Blair himself, given him a chance to deny the lies you and Wanda have made up about him.'

'They are not lies, Eilidh,' he said wearily. 'I only wish they were.'

'My name isn't Eilidh,' she muttered, still looking down at her hands which were clasped together tightly on her knees. 'It's Helen.'

'Eilidh is Gaelic for Helen. My grandmother was called Helen and my grandfather who came from the Hebrides and could speak Gaelic used to call her Eilidh. It means "light", a light shining in the darkness, I've always assumed.' He leaned closer to her and stroked the softly shining swathe of blonde hair which fell against her temple and her cheek. His knuckle brushed against her cheek and she jerked back from that gentle unexpected caress, her head lifting sharply, her eyes encountering the intense blue stare of his. 'You are well named, Eilidh,' he said softly. 'And you've come here a light to lighten my darkness.'

Suddenly she felt a strange tension, an awareness of him she hadn't felt before. She felt she was being pulled towards him. The feeling was electrifying and for Helen, who was still somewhat ignorant about sexual affinity, that spark of attraction which so often happens unexpectedly between two people who have never met before, it was frightening. Fighting off the desire to touch his cheek and then perhaps to slide her fingers through the silky strands of the dark hair which had slipped forward over his brow, she withdrew quickly, hiding behind the defence of her sharp tongue.

'I knew Magnus means great, but I don't think you're well named,' she remarked acidly. 'There's nothing great about deceiving a woman into coming here, forcing her to stay here and then ... to add insult to injury, sexually harassing her!'

Magnus drew back from her as if she had in fact hit him and his eyes narrowed warily.

'And when have I sexually harassed you?' he demanded with a touch of haughtiness as if he were insulted in his turn by what she had said.

'When you kissed me in the kitchen.'

'Good grief!' he exclaimed, and getting suddenly to his feet paced away from her into the shadows and back again to stand in front of her and frown down at her. 'You call a kiss like that sexual harassment? Ha!' His head went back as he laughed scornfully. 'Oh, Eilidh, you don't know what you're talking about,' he said, and with a lithe twist he sat down beside her on the sofa, so close she had to shift away from him into the corner beside the wide stuffed arm because his hard muscular thigh had pressed against hers— either by accident or on purpose, she couldn't be sure; so close that her senses, which for some reason were alive and tingling in a way she had never experienced before, were almost over- whelmed by the pulsing warmth of his lean body, by the scents of his hair and skin, by the blueness of his eyes, and the curve of his lips.

'You didn't have to kiss me,' she argued weakly.

'Agreed,' he murmured, moving closer to her. 'I didn't *have* to. But I wanted to and so I did.'

'You kissed me against my will,' she muttered, staring down at her hands again. They were gripping each other tightly. 'I didn't invite you to kiss me, so it was sexual harassment. You did it to annoy me.' She turned her head to give him an accusing glare, then wished she hadn't because he was much closer to her than she had realised.

'I did it because I couldn't help it,' he replied, his voice still soft. 'I did it to find out what you're really like behind that act you put on of being a cool, liberated type of woman about to indulge in an affair with another woman's husband.'

Across the small space which separated them his eyes challenged her and she looked away quickly, disconcerted again. What had he found out when he had kissed her? Slowly and inevitably her glance was drawn to him again. He was sitting half turned towards her, one knee resting on the sofa cushion, one hand resting on the back of the sofa, and he was watching her, a glimmer of amusement in his eyes, his lips curving in a slight half tender, half mocking smile, almost as if he knew about the confusion that was raging suddenly within her.

The feeling that she had seen him somewhere before leapt up. His lean face with its prominent high cheekbones, romantically hollow cheeks, bold straight nose, firm yet sensually curved lips, stubbornly jutting chin and above all the intensely blue eyes, deep set under the broad brow, were all vaguely familiar.

'Is Magnus your first name or your last?' she asked.

'First.' He moved away a little, out of the light shed by the standard lamp so that his face was in the shadow. 'Why do you ask?' he asked warily.

'I've this feeling I've met or seen you before somewhere. Have I?' Now she was leaning towards him, peering at him, trying to see his face more clearly.

But he wasn't looking in her direction any more, and she experienced a wild and rather frightening feeling that he wasn't there at all; that only a puppet was lolling on the sofa beside her; a handsome man puppet, dressed in dark clothing, with lax arms and legs and empty unseeing eyes who wouldn't move until she pulled the strings.

'Magnus!' she said sharply.

'Mmm?' To her great relief he moved and turned his head to look at her. Even in the shadow his eyes seemed to blaze with a bright blue light.

'Please, tell me,' she said. 'Have I ever seen or met you before today.'

'Not as far as I know,' he replied slowly. 'Unless you've. . . .' He broke off and his eyes were hidden momentarily as heavy lids fringed by black lashes dropped over them and he frowned. Then he looked at her again and smiled, a wide white smile that mocked her, but very gently. 'Unless you've met or seen me in your dreams, Eilidh,' he went on softly, shifting closer to her again. 'But I do know I haven't seen or met you before. I'd have remembered you if I had.' His voice deepened and the expression in his eyes was frankly sensual as their glance slanted down to her mouth. 'I would have remembered the sweetness of your lips, the fine texture of your skin, the shine of your hair. Oh, yes, Eilidh, I would have remembered you,' he whispered, leaning closer but not touching her.

'But today I have met you for the first time, and kissing you in the kitchen was quite an experience, one I would like to repeat, here and now.'

'No,' she murmured, but not very strongly, because she was mesmerised again by the magic of his voice and eyes.

'Yes,' he retorted, laughing a little and stretching an arm in front of her to rest his hand on the arm of the sofa, effectively trapping her in the corner.

'I . . . think you must be drunk,' she accused weakly, leaning back as far away from him as she could. She dared not let him kiss her again. She dared not let him find out too much about her.

'If I am it's with being close to you,' he whispered, leaning even closer but still not touching her. 'Let's kiss and be friends, Eilidh. Let's improve on that first experience, go further than that first sweet kiss of recognition and get to know each other better. We're going to be here together for at least two days, so why not make it a time to remember?'

'But I don't want to be kissed,' she protested, acknowledging to herself that she was lying. Now that his lips were within an inch of hers she was longing to feel them pressed against hers.

'I don't believe you, I don't believe you one little bit,' he mocked, and his slightly parted lips swooped to hers.

Warm, tasting a little of the whisky he had drunk, his lips moved subtly against the smoothness of hers and beneath that gentle yet provocative pressure her lips parted. A warm languorous glow spread through her and she lifted her arms about his neck to hold him closely, and they lay together against the back of the sofa and for a while time was lost, as, both drunk with desire, they kissed and kissed again, over and over, revelling in the taste, the feel and the smell of each other.

Never, not even with Blair, had Helen experienced such deep delight in being kissed and in kissing back. Until that moment she had always regarded kissing as silly and had more or less put up with Blair's attempts to make love to her, recognising it was something he felt he had to do and never realising that she was supposed to feel anything. But now it was as if as soon as Magnus's lips and hands touched her the delicate film of ice which covered her emotions at all times cracked and melted and passion poured forth, sweeping away all her inhibitions.

His breath was sweet and laced with whisky in her mouth. Against her cheeks, her throat and the cleft between her breasts his lips pressed in featherlight kisses. Responding to the caress of his fingers, her body arched taut and twanging like an archer's bow. She lifted her chin, to look at him again, wanting to know if kissing her made him feel the same way that kissing him made her feel. The slanted lamplight struck a deep dense blue from under the black sweep of his lashes. His lips, still parted from kissing her, were full and soft. Glints of gold glittered in the darkness of his ruffled hair. Helen had thought him attractive when seen at a distance, but now seen at close quarters, half drugged as she was with the demands of desire, he seemed to her to be the epitome of manly beauty, and she felt the surge of a new emotion; a craving to possess such a man, to make him hers for ever.

'You see, Eilidh, you do want to be kissed,' he whispered, stroking the hair away from her throat with gentle fingers. 'You do want to be made love to, and you want to make love to me just as surely as I want to make love to you.'

'But I don't understand,' she murmured, touching him too, tracing the provocative curve of his lower lip with her fingertips. 'We've only just met and . . . and we're not in love.'

'Aren't we?' The blue eyes smiled dazzlingly into hers, blinding her with their blazing brilliance. 'How do you know we're not? What is this we feel for each other if it isn't love of some sort?'

Taking a handful of her silky hair, he pulled it across his face, drawing some of it between his parted lips, and the sight of his tongue tasting the strands shocked Helen, at the same time arousing in her a new eroticism that swelled within her, demanding some sort of outlet. Moaning a little with a craving for she knew not what, she kissed his mouth while he was still tasting her hair, and from then on, their faces cloaked by the silver-gilt curtain of the straight silky stuff, they kissed even more deeply, became even more entangled with each other.

Magnus was right, she did want to make love to him just as surely as he wanted to make love to her. This feeling, like fire in her loins, was sexual desire, a longing which could only be satisfied in one way, by complete union with him, the person who had aroused it so exquisitely and expertly. And it would be exquisite and perfect with him, she guessed instinctively, because he was strong yet tender, disciplined yet easy, his hands controlling her slender body, playing upon it subtly as they might play a musical instrument, drawing from it a response which was stronger than her will.

And that was all she knew about him after all, this tantalising stranger who was teaching her something he knew about herself which she hadn't known until now, that she could be dominated by passion, whether it was her own or his.

A stranger. He was a stranger, about whom she still knew nothing except that his first name was Magnus, so how could she let him do this to her? How could she even contemplate going all the way with him and reaching passionate fulfilment with him? How could she go against her own moral code and do something with him that she had never even considered doing with Blair whom she was supposed to be in love with?

'Ah, no, no!' she cried out suddenly, twisting away from him. 'I can't do it! I don't know who you are ... and ... and I'm not in love with you.'

Sitting on the edge of the sofa, her back turned to him so that he wouldn't see the tears that were scalding her eyes or the trembling of her lips, she fastened the buttons of her blouse that he had undone. After being so close to complete surrender to desire withdrawal was proving to be very painful. Even her fingers were shaking. Behind her she could hear Magnus dragging in deep breaths as if he was also having difficulty in coming down from a trip induced by some hallucinatory drug and when he spoke his voice was husky, the words a little slurred.

'Why the sudden display of virtue?' he jeered. 'You were going to do it with Blair, and he's a married man.'

'I've told you already that I wasn't going to. . . .' she began to retort, turning on him angrily, her eyes blazing with tawny fire through the tears, and breaking off when she saw the cynical twist of his lips, the expression of disbelief in his eyes. He had changed again. The tender, passionate lover had become a world-weary, disillusioned man.

'If you weren't going to make love with Blair, and share his bed, why the hell were you going away with him?' he demanded, rising to his feet and going over to the small table beside the armchair. Picking up the decanter, he took out the stopper and poured more whisky into the glass.

'To ... to have a quiet holiday, a few days together where no one would know us, where we wouldn't be watched all the time and reported upon.'

'You really believe that was all it was going to be—a few quiet days, taking long country walks, perhaps, admiring the scenery and then going to your separate rooms at night?' he remarked scornfully. He flopped down in the armchair again, drank some of the whisky. 'Well, you can be sure that wasn't the sort of holiday Blair would have in mind at all,' he added, his glance drifting over her from head to foot. 'If he'd wanted that sort of holiday he would never have invited someone like you, Eilidh, you can be sure of that,' he added softly.

'Oh, I can see you've made up your mind about me and nothing I say is going to change it,' she retorted, bounding to her feet. 'Just because I've been friendly with Blair you've assumed I'm ... I'm promiscuous and that I sleep with any man who invites me to sleep with him. Well, I'm not! I've never wanted to make love with any man. ...' Realising she was about to say 'until now', she broke off confusedly and swung away from him, turning her back on him again in case he saw the rush of colour to her face. 'Never. Never,' she insisted, and turned towards him again, standing straight and proud, her hands in the pockets of her tweed jacket, her glance slanting down at him disdainfully. 'Do you hear?'

'I hear you all right, but that doesn't mean to say I believe you,' he drawled. 'You wanted to make love with me just now on that sofa.'

'I . . . I. . . . you took advantage,' she accused in a whisper.

'Maybe I did, but you didn't have to respond,' he retorted, then finished off the whisky and set the glass down. 'Oh, go away, Eilidh,' he added wearily, pouring more whisky. 'Go away and hide somewhere. The castle is big enough for us both to stay here without seeing each other, if that's the way you want it to be. And you don't have to lock your bedroom door. I won't be "taking advantage of you", as you call it, again tonight.'

Helen hesitated, watching him pick up the glass and drink from it.

'I hope you're not going to drink all that whisky tonight,' she said stiffly.

'What's it to you if I do?' he retorted. 'Are you a would-be reformer as well as a virgin?' he added nastily.

'I hate you!' she hissed at him, and turning on her heel marched from the room.

She went right upstairs to her bedroom, entered it and slammed the door shut behind her, hoping Magnus would hear the slam and know that she was angry. Across the dark room she stepped to the window and leaned her forehead against the pane to cool it. She could see nothing but rain-streaked blackness, could hear nothing but the roar and hiss of the unseen sea flinging itself against the reef of rocks in the small bay and the flute-like song of the wind.

She was trapped in a remote castle with a madman. Mad. Magnus was mad—he must be mad! Only a madman would entice a woman he didn't know to an isolated castle and then proceed to make love to her. And madness would account for his changeability, wouldn't it, for the way he had seemed like several different persons during the space of the few hours she had been with him?

Mad, bad and dangerous to know. She had read that somewhere. Frowning, she tried to remember. A poet had written it. But which poet? Ah, it was coming to her now, a memory of studying the Romantic poets in English Literature at school and reading about the infamous Lord Byron and his affair with Lady Caroline Lamb. It hadn't been a poet—it had been Lady Caroline herself, frantic and bitter after Byron had ended the affair. And then she had revenged herself on him by using him as the model for the hero-villain of her book *Glenarvon*, discrediting him in the eyes of the reading public.

Well, Magnus was mad, he must be to behave the way he had, impersonating Blair and making her come to this island. He was bad because he told lies and drank too much whisky. And he was dangerous to know—at least it was dangerous for her to know him, because he had the ability to change her from a cool collected person in charge of her emotions and knowing where she was going into a woman who could be overcome by her emotions; because he could make love so tenderly and expertly, arousing in her sensations she had read about but had always believed were beyond her experience. In an hour filled with purely sensual pleasure he had taught her what it was like to want a man and to want him in particular.

She groaned and pressed her head harder against the window pane as if by doing so she could obliterate the memory of his kisses. Just remembering how he had touched her made her breasts harden and the ache of longing begin, low down. Why? Why had he made love to her? Had he really wanted her as he had said he did? Was he really attracted to her? How? How could he be attracted to her so quickly? Love, even physical love, needed time to grow, didn't it?

Magnus. Magnus who? Magnus what? She hadn't found out. She had been going to ask him what his last name was, thinking that if she knew it she would recognise who he was. But he had taken control of the conversation. Yes, that was what had happened. When she had asked him if she could have seen or met him before today he had started to make love to her with words at first, not giving her a chance to question him further.

She straightened up and stared at the rainswept window. Had he made love to her deliberately to distract her? Had he wanted to stop her from finding out who he really was? Probably. Her hands clenched at her sides and she gritted her teeth as she realised how easily he had been able to distract her from her purpose, and she wished she could think up some way to get even with him.

Anger not just with Magnus but also with herself for having been so weak and having responded to his lovemaking pulsed through her, and turning away from the window she switched on the bedside lamp and began to undress. She would go to bed, even though it was only ten o'clock. She would get a good night's rest, get up early in the morning and find some way of escaping from the island. Finding her nightdress and dressing gown, she put them on and then visited the bathroom next door. As she returned to the bathroom she noticed how quiet the castle was except for the battering of the wind against walls and windows. Where did Magnus sleep? she wondered. *I don't want to know. I don't want to know*, she answered herself fiercely, and hurrying into the bedroom she closed the door firmly and finding a key in the lock turned it. Although Magnus had said she didn't need to lock it to keep him out she didn't trust him.

Once she was in bed she tried very hard to make her mind a blank, to blot him from her thoughts, but she couldn't. It seemed that he had taken over, blotting out her memories of Blair even.

Who was he? A friend of Wanda Murray, who was Blair's wife. What sort of friend would Wanda have? Other singing stars? Members of the rock groups who accompanied her? Was that what Magnus did? Was he a guitarist or a drummer, or even another singer? Was that why he seemed familiar to her?

She tried to remember which groups had accompanied Wanda on her records and to fit them to the groups she had seen herself over the past few years while she had been emerging from adolescence into womanhood. She had seen them either on television or in photographs in magazines, or a few times in person when she had gone to rock concerts. But none of the members of the groups had been tall and graceful, with brilliant blue eyes.

She fell asleep while she was still struggling to solve the problem of Magnus's identity, and when she wakened the room was full of light, the pearl-grey light of early morning, and the wind seemed to have abated. She looked at her watch. It was six-thirty. Perhaps now would be a good time to leave before Magnus was up and about. Getting out of bed, she padded over to the window and stood for a moment transfixed by the beauty of the view.

The sea was calm, stretching like silvery grey silk to a distant clearly defined horizon. Scattered islands loomed, some high and mountainous, some low and flat, merely shelves of rock just showing above the surface of the water. Below, in the small bay in front of the castle, reefs of red rocks glowed against pale sand where big white and grey gulls stalked about seeking for food in pools.

The storm was over, the sea was calm. She would go to the jetty again and hope to find some way of signalling to the Macleishes' cottage. Perhaps she might see a fishing boat going by and be able to attract the fisherman's attention. Anyway, she was going to leave the castle. She couldn't possibly spend all day in it, knowing that Magnus was somewhere in it too.

Quickly she dressed in the clothes she had worn the previous day, packed her suitcase and left the bedroom. She tiptoed along the landing and down the stairs and entered the kitchen warily. It was just as she had left it the previous evening. She picked up her raincoat and put it on, then left by the back door. In a few minutes she was walking across the moorland, stepping carefully to avoid the boggy patches. The air was soft and damp, singing with the sound of many small streams, and by the time she reached the pinewood the sun had broken through the thin

grey gauze clouds and was flushing everything
with rosy light.

When she reached the jetty she was short of
breath and her suitcase felt as if it weighed a ton.
The little bay was smooth and unruffled, reflecting
pale clouds and patches of blue sky perfectly.
Across the swirling water of the narrow strait the
sunlit walls of the Macleishes' cottage twinkled.
Helen walked right to the end of the jetty and
dropped her suitcase. If only she had something to
wave that would attract attention! But they would
only see her if they were looking, she thought
dejectedly.

She turned and looked back at the land curving
behind the bay, hoping to see the motorboat
washed up on the crescent of yellow sand. Her
glance followed the beach right round to the cliffs
which protected the bay from the north. Tucked
under the shelter of the jumble of red rocks was
the grey shape of a boathouse. Her eyes narrowed.
Was that a boat, painted white, lying beside the
nearest wall of the shed?

Suddenly she was off and running back along
the jetty, turning right along a path which wound
through reeds and clumps of sea-pinks. Terns,
small white birds, disturbed by her approach,
soared up into the air before her, squealing
angrily.

At last the walls of the boathouse loomed before
her. They were green with moss and half hidden by
overgrown bushes. In the long grass lay a small
white-painted dinghy, its flat bottom upwards. It
was the sort Helen recognised from her days of
sailing with her father on the Solway Firth, often
pulled by bigger yachts as tenders for getting
ashore.

Triumph surged through her. She had found a way of escape! If there were oars and rowlocks she would be able to row across the strait, to her car. In little more than an hour she would be on her way, speeding south.

CHAPTER THREE

TAKING hold of the rail of the dinghy, Helen lifted it and pushed the boat over on to its bottom. Where it had been covered by the boat the grass was white and yellow. Two oars lay there, the varnished wood from which they were made gleaming gold in the sunlight. She examined the inside of the dinghy. It had three thwarts, one on the bow, one across the centre and another in the stern. Tied to the centre thwart were two rowlocks.

Since the dinghy was made apparently from marine plywood it wasn't as heavy as it would have been if it had been a more traditional boat and made from heavy planks of wood, and she was able to drag it off the grass and on to the beach, close to the water. When she had done that she returned to the jetty to fetch her suitcase. By the time she was back at the dinghy she was hot and breathless, so she took off her raincoat, folded it up and put it in the bow thwart, then leaned for a while against the little boat, resting, watching the water lapping at the sand and occasionally looking over to the jetty in case Magnus appeared suddenly.

Putting the oars in the dinghy and her suitcase on the floor of it, she pushed the little boat bow first into the clear water and stepped into it. She sat in the middle of the centre thwart, and taking hold of the oars pushed against the beach with them, thrusting the dinghy farther out until it was afloat. Then she slid the oars into the rowlocks which she had fitted into the galvanised iron rings attached to the wooden rail of the boat and began to row, glad that she had learned how at an early age.

She was about twelve yards away from the shore and was almost out into the strait when she realised that her feet were wet. Glancing down, she saw that about two inches of water was slopping about in the bottom of the dinghy. Deciding that some of it had slopped over the bow when it had hit one of the small waves that were rippling into the bay, she rowed on, pulling less strongly on the oars. She judged that the distance to the mainland was about a mile and a half to two miles, and if the little boat was going to take water over its bow she would have to row more carefully, more gently, so it would take her longer than the hour she had expected.

A few minutes later water slithered over the tops of her shoes and into them, completely submerging her feet, and yet she was sure no water had come over the bow. Lifting her feet out of the water, she rested them on the stern thwart. The position wasn't comfortable and it made rowing more difficult, so she lowered them again into the water.

She was out of the bay and the jetty was growing smaller and the dark pines and the rock-scattered tawny moorland behind them seemed to be growing higher and higher when she heard the shout. A figure was running along the jetty, a man dressed in a bright yellow jacket. Magnus. Stopping at the end of the jetty, he waved his arms at her above his head, then cupping his hands about his mouth he shouted again.

'The dinghy has a hole in it,' she heard quite clearly. 'Come back, Eilidh! Come back at once!'

So that was why the boat was filling with water. Helen stopped rowing and looked down. The water was halfway up the sides of the boat now and her suitcase was almost covered. Pulling hard on the right oar, she tried to turn the dinghy, but it was too water-logged for her to make it turn, added to which she was out in a strong tidal current and the boat was being swept slowly but surely along, not towards the mainland or towards Carroch, but towards the wider expanse of the Sound of Jura.

Tempted to stand up, take off her jacket and dive into the water, Helen seemed to hear her father's instructions about what to do when a boat was in danger of sinking or capsizing repeating in her mind. *Stay with the boat, always stay with the boat. Hold on to it, because it will float. So will an oar or part of a mast. Hang on to any piece of wood that you can.*

Suddenly she realised that she would have to get out of the boat if she wanted it to keep floating. Moving to one side of it, she tipped the rail under and fell into the water with a splash. At once the current caught at her, trying to whirl her away from the boat which, as she had hoped, had turned over and was now floating upside down. As she passed it she flung herself forward and managed to throw herself on top of its flat bottom. Breathless, half-choked by the salt water she had swallowed when she had fallen in the water, she lay there, only just above the surface of the deadly swirling water, but at least not in it.

How much time passed before she heard the distinctive roar of the motorboat's engine she couldn't be sure, but she heard it with a feeling of incredulity and looked round to see its black bow forging towards her, wings of white spray flying up on either side of it. Behind the windshield was a man in a yellow jacket.

When the motorboat was alongside the dinghy Magnus put the engine in neutral and leaned over the side, stretching out a hand to her.

'Give me your hand and I'll pull you in closer so that I can lift you aboard,' he ordered.

Helen did as he told her and was glad to feel his hand, warm and strong, close around hers. When the dinghy was close to the motorboat she knelt up and he lifted her, holding her under the armpits, and with a little push against the bottom of the dinghy she was up and over the side of the motorboat.

Magnus pushed her into the passenger seat, put the engine in gear, swung the steering wheel, opened the throttle and headed back towards the jetty in the bay. Sweeping back her wet hair and feeling uncomfortably clammy, Helen looked around the boat. It was the same one in which he had taken her to Carroch the previous day, the one she had believed had been washed away during the storm.

'Where did you find the boat?' she demanded, turning to him. 'Was it washed ashore somewhere?'

He slanted her a bright glance over his shoulder. His face was very pale, she noticed, and his mouth was set in a grim tight line.

'You could have been drowned,' he said, his voice grating. 'You bloody little fool! Why didn't you check the dinghy to make sure it was seaworthy before you launched it?'

Why hadn't she? Because she had been too excited by her find, too pleased to have discovered a way of escaping, to take the time to check the dinghy for holes. She glanced over the sun-shimmering water to the mainland which was going farther and farther away again as they approached the island jetty. The whitewashed walls of the Macleish cottage glimmered yellow with reflected sunlight, seeming to mock her, and the water of the strait swirled by relentlessly, blue and silver. Magnus was right, she could have drowned, and if he hadn't followed her she would have been swept right past Carroch by now, would be in the wide expanse of the Sound of Jura. She owed him her life.

The motorboat swung in behind the sheltering wall of the jetty and nudged up to the steps. Magnus put the engine in neutral.

'Get out,' he ordered. 'And take the rope with you.'

'Please take me to the mainland,' she said, turning to him.' 'Please!'

His blue glance was wintry as it flicked over her wet hair and drenched clothing.

'No, not now. Not yet. You need a bath and a change of clothes,' he replied coldly. 'Here, take the rope and get out.'

'Oh, my clothes!' she groaned. 'My suitcase sank . . . and my handbag with everything in it, my car keys, money—everything! Oh, what am I going to do?'

'You're going to go back to the castle with me, you're going to have a hot bath, change your clothes and then have breakfast,' said Magnus clearly and concisely. 'Heaven knows I never thought you'd be such a damned nuisance when I agreed to prevent you from going away with Blair. Now will you bloody well get out or do I have to heave you ashore?'

He was very angry, boiling with rage, and he wasn't pretending. There was nothing counterfeit about the fury glaring at her out of his eyes.

'You don't have to be so...so abusive,' she retorted.

'I said get out!' he roared at her, and she turned at once and slipping and sliding in her wet crepe-soled shoes scrambled over the rail of the motorboat, taking the rope with her, and hurried up the steps of the jetty. Behind her Magnus cut the engine, then leapt ashore and followed her up the steps. Taking the rope from her, he looped it through an iron ring. Standing shivering now with delayed shock as well as with cold from the water which had soaked her clothes, she watched him tie the rope deftly.

'I hope that knot will hold the boat and it doesn't get washed away again,' she stuttered.

He didn't answer her but, straightening up, took hold of her arm, grasping it tightly just above the elbow, and urged her along the jetty, and there was nothing she could do about it. She was too wet and cold, too shocked by her recent near-drowning, to make any sort of protest.

In spite of the sunshine and the mild air flowing about her, in spite of the beauty of the scenery around her now fully revealed in bright daylight, the gold, green and soft blue of islands, sea and sky, Helen could not enjoy her return walk to the castle. Walking in shoes that had become saturated with sea-water was not easy, and several times she would have stopped to catch her breath and rest if Magnus hadn't kept on pushing her along, so that by the time they were crossing the garden and approaching the castle she was reviling him silently and secretly as a cruel sadist who delighted in inflicting pain on others. Not even when they were in the house did he let go of her arm, but marched her across the kitchen and up the stairs to the bathroom.

Flinging open the door, he pushed her into the room, not even letting go of her when he bent to put the plug in the drain of the old-fashioned free-standing bath and to turn on the taps.

'Now get those clothes off,' he ordered, turning to her. 'Or do I have to do that for you too?'

'No, no, you don't have to do anything for me,' she retorted, her sturdy spirit of independence suddenly asserting itself again and shaking off the dejection and shock which the failure of her attempt to escape had plunged her into. 'But . . . but what will I wear instead?' she demanded, managing to free herself from his grasp.

'I'll find you something,' he replied, and strode out of the room.

She was struggling with the zip on her pants—it seemed to have been seized up by salt water—when he returned carrying a rich-looking crimson and grey striped man's dressing gown, made from velour, and a big fluffy white towel monogrammed in red with two initials, an M intertwined with an S.

'What's the matter now?' he demanded roughly, tossing the gown and the towel down on a stool.

'Nothing much. I can't get the zip undone, that's all,' she muttered, giving the tab of the zip another tug. Immediately it broke off. 'Oh, darn!' she cried.

White steam was swirling about them and the bath was almost full of water. After giving her another exasperated glance Magnus stepped over and turned off the taps, then turned back to her.

In a swift lithe movement he knelt beside her, grasped hold of her pants at the top of the opening with both hands and pulled hard. The zip ripped apart.

'Anything else?' he queried silkily, as he straightened up.

'No, no, thank you—I can manage now,' she said in a stifled voice.

'I hope you can,' he drawled dryly, going to the doorway. 'Try not to drown in the bathtub,' he added mockingly, and went away.

After soaking for a while in the hot water Helen got out of the bath, dried herself and put on the velour robe. Luxuriously soft, it caressed her skin which was still glowing from the rubbing she had given it. It was like being touched by Magnus, she thought fancifully, and was amazed at herself for having such an erotic thought. The sleeves of the robe were wide, curving over her shoulder and arms like a shawl. There was a tie belt and the skirt flowed out and down to her feet. On Magnus, she guessed, it reached only halfway down his legs. The breast pocket was adorned with the same monogram as the towel, this time in black.

An M interwoven with an S. In the slightly steamed-up bathroom mirror Helen watched her reflection trace the letters with a fingertip. M for Magnus. S for what? She searched her mind for a Scottish name beginning with S and came up with two: Stuart and Sanderson. Although it didn't have to be a Scottish name, she supposed, because Magnus himself, when he had stopped being Blair or the wild islander, didn't seem or sound to be Scottish. But then he changed so often it was difficult to know what he was really like.

She emptied the bath, picked up her wet clothes

and left the room to go downstairs to the kitchen. Magnus wasn't there, but he had been there, because on the draining board beside the sink were the dishes he had used when he had breakfasted.

Helen looked at her wet clothing. She would have liked to have washed everything and wrung the salt water out before hanging it up to dry. The tweed jacket was in a terrible mess and being made wholly of wool would probably shrink. The pants too were unwearable and the zip was destroyed. Eventually she decided to wash only the blouse and the underwear in the sink and to hang everything on the old-fashioned drying rack which was attached to the ceiling and could be raised and lowered by ropes on pulleys.

She had made and eaten some breakfast and had gone into the lounge and was searching the bookshelves for something to read when Magnus came into the room. He was dressed differently this morning. A blue knit leisure shirt open at the neck and halfway down his chest clung to the muscular shape of his chest and dark blue denim jeans hugged his hips and powerful thighs. He was a vigorous presence in the room, having about him a sort of charisma which drew Helen's glance to him all the time and even made her want to go up to him and touch him, make him notice her. He was a threat to her peace of mind, dangerous for her to know, and it took all her self-control to stay sitting where she was on a chair by the bookshelves and to leaf through a book she had taken down; to pretend she couldn't care less if he were in the room or not.

'I hope you haven't any more escapades planned for today,' he said coldly, advancing towards her and standing over her, his arms folded across his chest. 'It's a good thing I saw you leaving the castle this morning and followed you, or you'd be halfway to Ireland by now, a horrid bloated body being turned over and over by the waves.'

'Oh, don't, don't!' she cried, dropping the book and covering her ears with her hands. 'I don't want to think about it!'

'Why did you do it?' he demanded, sitting down suddenly on the floor at her feet, crossing his legs and staring up at her. 'Did you really think you could row to the mainland in that little apology for a dinghy?'

'Yes, I did.' She lowered her hands to her lap and stealthily pulled the robe together across her knees to cover them and her legs. Where Magnus was sitting he would have a good view of them if the robe's opening slipped apart. 'I'm quite used to handling boats, and the water was calm.'

'Or so it seemed,' he jibed. 'That strait, the Carroch Strait, is deceptive. Like many other stretches of water about here, like the Dorus Mhor, off Crinan, and the Corrievrechan between Scarba and Jura, it flows over an uneven bottom and has a strong current, creating whirlpools. You need either a hefty engine like there is in the motorboat or a fishing boat to cross it. You'd never have made it in the dinghy even if it hadn't had a hole in it, and in bad weather like last night that strait is impassable.' He paused, then asked in a gentler voice, 'Eilidh, why did you try to get to the mainland by yourself? Why didn't you wait and ask me to take you over?'

'I . . . I . . . I. . . .' she stammered, then stopped, looked right at him and blurted suddenly, 'Because I wanted to get away from you.'

There was an uneasy silence while they stared at

each other. Magnus looked away first, down at his hands which were linked together and lying lax between his crossed legs. He didn't say anything, but his whole face seemed to tense and Helen had the impression that she had hurt him in some way.

'Oh, it . . . it wasn't because . . . because I don't like you,' she went on hurriedly, saying more than she had intended. 'But I didn't want to come here and I don't want to stay here for another day. If I could have found the motorboat I'd have been across by now. I'd be in my car and on the way home.'

'No, you wouldn't,' he retorted, looking up. 'Unless of course you can start a boat's engine without a key,' he added dryly, his eyes glinting with mockery.

'Oh, I never thought of that,' she admitted lamely, annoyed with herself because she hadn't. Usually she thought of everything, being of a scientific turn of mind she was very methodical in her planning. 'But you haven't told me where you found the motorboat yet,' she added. 'Where was it washed up?'

'Never mind where I found it,' he replied. 'I did, and just in time to rescue you from a watery grave.' In a lithe graceful movement which was hardly noticeable, it was so fluid, he kneeled in front of her, resting his hands on the arms of her chair. 'You know Eilidh, if you'd drowned, I'd have been very upset.' His voice softened and deepened and his eyes were dark with some emotion. He looked as if he were tortured by regret. 'I brought you here, so I feel responsible for you, and if you'd drowned it would have been on my conscience for ever—and I've enough on my conscience as it is.' He paused, frowning. 'But you couldn't be wishing more than I am that I hadn't enticed you to come here,' he whispered.

'Then if you feel like that, why don't you take me over to the mainland?' she asked, staring at him in bewilderment. This was another, different man from the man of yesterday. Was this the real Magnus?

'Dressed like that?' he queried, his amused glance sliding over his own soft luxurious robe. 'Or in shrunk, soaking wet clothes? Oh, no, Eilidh,' he leaned closer to her, 'you can't leave today.'

'Tomorrow, then,' she said, pushing her advantage. 'Will you take me over to my car tomorrow?' Her shoulders slumped suddenly and she let out a sigh of exasperation. 'Oh, but what will be the use?' she moaned. 'The keys are in my handbag and that's at the bottom of the sea. Could you— do you think you could start the car for me without keys . . . that is if we can get into it? I locked the doors too.'

'I might be able to. Or Archie might be able to help you.' Magnus spoke vaguely, still staring at her as if he had never seen her before.

'Will you promise then to take me over in the motorboat?' she whispered. 'Please!' she touched him at last, placing a hand on one of his forearms. Under her fingers the hair-sprinkled skin was warm and silky and the muscle tensed in reaction to her touch.

'It's a rule of mine never to make promises,' he said softly. 'That way I don't have to break any. Who knows, tomorrow I might be only too glad to get rid of you and will be very willing to take you to the mainland. On the other hand, you might find that when tomorrow comes you won't want to go and I might find I don't want to let you go. By then we might be so in love with each other we won't want to part.'

The blue eyes smiled into hers and she felt again that weak jelly-like feeling in her legs. Heat flooded through her, seeming to melt her bones. She was helpless as she had been in the dangerous waters of Carroch Strait, being swept along now by a strong tide of eroticism which threatened to engulf her. Alarmed by the feeling, she leaned back away from him.

'I think you're quite mad—quite mad,' she whispered.

'I think I am too,' he agreed. His hands slid up her arms slowly to her shoulders, leaving delicious tingles wherever they touched her. His fingers stroked her throat gently. His blue eyes looked deeply into hers. 'The lunatic and the lover are of the same breed,' he murmured, 'and I'm mad with wanting you. Last night I couldn't sleep for thinking of you and wanting you.' His fingers slid down her throat and slipped under the edges of the velour robe. Against her cool, still slightly moist skin his hands were warm. 'And from the feel of you I know you want me,' he added softly, and bending his head he kissed her throat and her breast, everywhere his hands had been.

'Oh,' sighed Helen, swaying towards him, her lips parting, 'what are you doing to me?'

'I'm loving you,' he whispered. 'Showing you how glad I am you didn't drown. Ah, Eilidh, if you had drowned life would have been hell for me as I spent the rest of it searching the sea and the shores of the islands for you.'

'But I didn't drown. I'm here, and I'm alive and well,' she comforted him, letting the dangerous tide of sexual excitement carry her along now, pressing herself against him, regardless of the fact that the robe was untied and falling away from her soft white body. 'You rescued me, I owe you my life.' Under her urgent seeking hands his ruffled spray-damp hair twisted and sprang like something alive as she stroked it. 'And I thank you with all my heart for coming to my rescue. I . . . I want to love you to show you how much I'm glad you saw me leave this morning and followed me.'

He lifted his head and their lips met in a long, deeply demanding kiss. Her head spinning, Helen surrendered, with a voluptuousness which would have surprised her if she had been able to observe herself objectively, to the caress of his long lean fingers. Then with a groan of agony, as if he had been driven over the edge of madness by the feel of her, Magnus pulled her from the chair to the soft silkiness of the sealskin hearthrug until she was lying there with him and he was kissing her again and again, sweet-tasting, drugging kisses which obliterated all thoughts of past and future, until all that mattered to both of them were the present sunlit moments in the quiet room and the satisfaction of their mutual desire to possess each other.

Through the drooping fringes of her eyelashes Helen watched him pull off his shirt, and her hands reached out eagerly to caress his bareness, her fingers worshipping the broad slant of his shoulders, the fine moulding of bones gleaming like ivory through the sunbronzed skin of his neck, sliding down over the velvet smoothness of his back, tormenting hollows, until with another exclamation of passion he pressed against her, holding her tightly in his arms so that she could feel the urgency of his desire thrusting against her thighs.

'I didn't know loving someone would be like this,' she whispered. 'I didn't know it could be so sudden and happen between two strangers.'

'We're not strangers, Eilidh. We've always known each other. We just hadn't met,' Magnus murmured fancifully.

'But I don't know your last name.'

He stiffened a little and raised his head from her breast where his lips had been marauding the soft white skin. His glance was lazily arrogant.

'Does it matter?' he retorted lightly. 'As Shakespeare put it, "What's in a name? That which we call a rose by any other name would smell as sweet." We don't need to know names, it's what we feel that matters. Here and here.' He rested a hand lightly on her left breast, then let it slide gently downwards, and, once again mesmerised by the way he was looking at her and touching her, Helen drew his head down so she could kiss him and gave in to the enjoyment of the delicious sensations which were flooding through her.

Then suddenly he was rolling away from her, twisting to his feet and grabbing his shirt from the floor.

'What is it?' she gasped, sitting up quickly, the heavy silk of her pale yellow hair falling straight over the smooth white curves of her shoulders and breasts.

'Someone is knocking at the kitchen door. Get that robe on,' he ordered crisply, turning his back to her as he zipped up his jeans and fastened the belt at his waist.

'Hello there, Magnus?' called out a loud

boisterous male voice from the kitchen. 'Magnus? Are you at home?'

With the velour robe about her shoulders, Helen stood up. She pushed her arms into the wide sleeves and tied the belt at her waist just in time. Heavy footsteps sounded on the stone floor of the kitchen and advanced into the hallway. His shirt on, raking fingers through his disordered hair but his feet bare, his socks lying like incriminating evidence by the hearthrug, Magnus went towards the half-open door of the lounge. He was too late to stop whoever had come to see him from entering the room. Snatching up the socks, Helen stepped over to the long window which looked over the bay, smoothing back her hair with one hand. Then she slipped each hand into the opposite sleeve of the robe, holding her arms folded in front of her, hiding the socks. She was, she discovered, shaking all over, and her heart was pounding and her cheeks were flushed as she realised how nearly she and Magnus had been seen making love in full daylight on the hearthrug.

'What on earth have you come here for?' Magnus's voice was gruff with anger.

'What else could I do but come in person?' retorted the loud male voice. 'There's no way I could contact you. By Jove, this is some place you've got here, Magnus,' the loud voice softened admiringly. 'But not easy of access. Took us quite a while to figure out how to get here.'

'Us?' queried Magnus sharply. 'You've brought someone with you?'

'I sure have. Marta Nielsen, the Swedish actress, and Leon Rossi, the film director.' The loud voice shouted loudly from the doorway. 'Hey, Marta, Leo! Come right through. He's here!'

Over her shoulder Helen looked at Magnus, wildly questioningly.

'Stay there,' he whispered at her, gesturing with one hand, before turning back to face the doorway as the man with the loud voice, who was tall and heavily built and was wearing a double-breasted pale grey suit and a brown and white striped shirt, stepped back into the lounge and was followed by two other people.

She's quite small, almost insignificant, thought Helen, as she stared at the well-known Swedish actress whom she had seen a couple of times in rather heavy psychological films. Marta Nielsen stared back, her attention caught and held by Helen's tall, slim figure silhouetted against the sunlit window.

'I hope we are not intruding,' she said politely, still looking at Helen.

'You are,' retorted Magnus with brutal frankness, then held out his right hand and smiled at Marta. 'But welcome to Carroch Castle just the same. I'm pleased to meet you at last.'

'Thank you,' said the actress, her own smile a faint curving of the lips that had tantalised so many of her fans. 'Coming to see you has been quite an adventure. You have a wonderful hideaway here. I am envious.' Her grey eyes glanced at Helen, who had half turned away to look out of the window. 'This is your wife?' she asked, gesturing towards Helen, who hearing the question, swung round to face the actress in alarm.

'Come and be introduced,' said Magnus, turning to smile at Helen. Tall and graceful, seeming completely at ease he stepped towards her and taking hold of her arm above the elbow urged her towards the others. Her hands were still hidden in the wide sleeves of the robe and his socks were still in her right hand. 'This is Eilidh, a friend of mine,' Magnus said. 'And Eilidh, I would like you to meet Marta Nielsen, Leo Rossi and Max Fiedler.'

Relieved that neither of the men nor Marta offered to shake hands with her, Helen smiled shyly and a little uncertainly, her eyes encountering the warm amused brown eyes of the bearded Italian film director.

'Hi, Eili . . . that's some name you have. Sorry I can't pronounce it,' said the ebullient Max Fiedler, grinning at her, his small black eyes glinting knowledgeably behind his thick-lensed glasses.

'It's a beautiful name,' said Marta. 'I suppose it is Scottish.' Her smile was gentle and the expression in her eyes kind and understanding, as if she knew exactly how embarrassed Helen was feeling.

'It's Gaelic for Helen,' Magnus said coolly.

'I think I prefer Helen,' said Leo Rossi charmingly. 'You will, I hope, excuse me, Helen, for bursting in on you and Magnus like this, but it is important that we discuss with him some business, and coming here to see him seemed to be the only way.' He turned to Magnus. 'Do you know we had to hire a fishing boat with its captain and mate to bring us here from Oban this morning? Making contact with you has proved to be expensive, my friend,' he added, laughing as he clapped Magnus in a friendly way on the shoulder. 'I hope the trip we have made is going to prove to have been worthwhile. The boat will wait for us to take us back later. For my part I'm glad the weather is calm. I am not a good sailor. What about you, Marta?'

Leo sat down beside the actress on the sofa. Max was already lounging in one of the big armchairs.

'I too am glad the weather is fine,' replied Marta serenely. 'All the way coming here we could see for miles and miles and the islands—the mountains, the sea looked so beautiful. I have been much in the Greek Islands, but I do not think the colours there are anything compared to the jewel-like quality of the colours here. It is all so unpolluted.'

'Go and make us some coffee and sandwiches,' Magnus whispered to Helen, letting go of her arm.

'Is this castle very old?' Marta asked.

'This tower was originally built in the fifteenth century, but of course it has been restored many times,' Magnus was replying as Helen, who was glad he had suggested that she should leave the room, excused herself and went to the kitchen.

Once she was in the kitchen she closed the door and collapsed on one of the chairs at the table. She wanted to laugh and cry all at once. She wanted to laugh at the way she and Magnus had hurriedly dressed themselves and had tried to appear unconcerned in front of the three people who had arrived so unexpectedly, but she wanted to cry too, with disappointment, because she and Magnus had been interrupted when they had been dizzy with delight, trapped in a spell of sensual pleasure, when they had been so close to the culmination of passion.

It had all happened so beautifully and naturally, and it had been an experience beyond her wildest dreams. For a few moments Magnus had done something for her that no other man had been able to do. Making love to her tenderly and expertly, he had freed her from the cold stiff shyness that had always imprisoned her warm and generous heart and her longing to love and be loved, and now she was his prisoner for ever, captivated completely by his gentle strength and his generosity as a lover.

But what now? Where did she go from that point of time in the lounge when she had begun to experience for the first time the joys of sensual pleasure? What would they have done, what would she and Magnus have said to each other if three strangers had not arrived? She drew her hands out of the wide sleeves of the dressing gown and looked at Magnus's socks still clutched in her hands and smiled, a rather trembling smile, as tears filled her eyes. Thank heavens the strangers hadn't arrived a few minutes earlier and found her and Magnus lying in each other's arms on the sealskin hearthrug! Yet none of them had seemed surprised to find her, dressed in what was obviously his dressing gown, branded with his initials . . . no, that wasn't quite right, she thought, frowning now. None of them had been surprised to find any woman with Magnus.

The thought disturbed her, arousing a new emotion, a feeling of jealousy because she guessed she wasn't the only woman in his life; wasn't the only woman he had made love to. Jumping to her feet, irritated with herself for allowing such a base and violent feeling to take over, she pushed the socks into a drawer in the dresser and finding a kettle filled it with water.

While she lit a burner on the gas cooker she considered the three people who had arrived. They all knew Magnus. Oh, it was true Marta Nielsen and Leo Rossi hadn't met Magnus before, but they knew of him. And Max Fiedler seemed to know him extremely well. A film actress, a film director and a . . . not knowing much about the film industry, she couldn't even begin to guess what Max Fiedler did for a living. He would be an actor, she supposed.

Then what was Magnus, and why had they come in a fishing boat to see him? Behind her the door to the hallway opened and she turned to look at it. Marta Nielsen was standing there.

'The bathroom?' queried the actress with a lift of her shapely mobile eyebrows.

'Upstairs, on the first landing. Second door on the right,' Helen replied.

'Thank you. I'll be back,' Marta made a grimace and jerked her head back in the direction of the lounge. 'They are talking money and contracts, and all that stuff bores me.'

Marta backed out and closed the door. Helen found a tray and set it with an embroidered traycloth she found in the drawer of the dresser. She found coffee mugs, a jar of instant coffee, milk and sugar, and she was making sandwiches when the door opened again and Marta returned.

'I do like this place,' said the actress, sitting down at the table. 'And I envy Magnus his possession of it.'

'Oh, but. . . .' Helen broke off, frowning as she turned to the cooker. The kettle was boiling. Had Magnus been lying again, saying the castle belonged to him? Or he lied to her when he had said the castle belonged to a relative of Blair's? No, that wasn't what he had said. He had said the castle belonged to a relative of his and she had assumed he had meant a relative of Blair's because at the time he had been pretending to be Blair.

'It's so exciting for me to meet him, too,' Marta went on, apparently not having noticed Helen's objection. 'Ever since I saw him act the part of Shelley some years ago in that T.V. series about the English Romantic poets I have hoped one day to meet Magnus Scott. Did you see the series, by any chance?'

Standing perfectly still at the cooker, staring at the steam coming out of the spout of the kettle, Helen forced herself to answer as casually as she could.

'Yes, I did.' She cleared her throat, turned off the burner and lifting the kettle went over to the table to pour boiling water in the coffee mugs. 'Are you going to act with him?'

'It is probable. Leo wants him for his next film. It's a story of romance and intrigue set in Italy at the time of Napoleon. It will give Leo a chance to include some of the beauties of his native land. I will play the part of an Austrian wife of an Italian count and . . . if he agrees . . . Magnus will be the English diplomat and courier who falls in love with me. Are you an actress too, Helen?'

'Me? Oh, no!'

'You have forgiven me, I hope, for the *faux pas* I made just now when I assumed you were Magnus's wife?' asked Marta.

'Yes, yes, of course I have.'

'I wouldn't have made such an assumption if Max hadn't said when we were coming here that he wouldn't be at all surprised if Magnus had got married secretly and had come to this island for his honeymoon. So naturally I thought, when we found you here with him in such intimate circumstances, that Max was right. But as soon as I heard your name, I knew I had made a mistake. Max had said that Magnus had been seen a lot

recently with a singer . . . a British recording star.'
Marta's high white forehead pleated as she made
an effort to remember and she pushed a hand at
her abundant soft brown hair which was coiled
into a rather untidy chignon on top of her head. 'I
think he said her name was Wanda. Yes, that is
right. Wanda Murray. You have heard of her,
perhaps?' Marta smiled at Helen across the table.

Helen, who had just lifted the tray to carry it
into the lounge, nearly dropped it. Quickly she set
it down.

'Yes, I have heard of her,' she said weakly. 'But
Magnus couldn't marry her. She's married already,
to a doctor.'

'Then Max must have made a mistake . . . about
the name, I mean,' said Marta, rising to her feet
and going over to open the door, 'or he's been
listening to gossip. He often does that and gets the
story all wrong.'

'Who is he? I mean, what does he do? Is he an
actor too?' asked Helen, lifting up the tray again.

'He's a film producer. In fact he produced the
last three films Magnus appeared in, and Magnus
is under contract to him, I believe.' Marta sighed
and rolled her eyes. 'He is not the pleasantest of
persons, but he knows how to raise money for
films and he knows how to market them. He is
very necessary to people like me, and Magnus and
Leo. Without him we would not have the
opportunity to reach the cinema-going public.'

Trying to appear calm and unconcerned, Helen
carried the tray into the lounge and set it down on
the coffee table in front of the sofa where both
Magnus and Leo were sitting. Max was striding up
and down the room, smoking a cigar and
apparently giving the other two men a lecture.

'Now the way I see it the only things that matter in this business are: one, a good story, and we've got that.' He swung round to glare down at Magnus. 'You've read it. You should have done by now—you've had the damned script long enough.' Not waiting for an answer, he continued with his pacing and his advice. 'Two,' he said, striking the second finger of his left hand with the first finger of his right hand. 'You have to have interesting casting, and in Marta and you,' he swung round to glare at Magnus again, 'that's if we can only get you to agree to do it, we have two of the best actors, who also happen to have the same photogenic presence of a Bergman or a Garbo, a Newman or a Redford—you come over good on the big screen and people will pay to go and see you. And three,' he struck the third finger of his left hand as he went on pacing, 'a good director, and Leo has proved time and time again that he's the best. It's the human element that makes a motion picture, not the technology, but unfortunately we can't do without that, and it's expensive, damned expensive.'

'I agree,' said Leo Rossi smoothly, smiling at Helen as she offered him a mug of coffee. 'It is expensive, but my point is that with new technology we're going to make the cost of a film much lower than it has been. Magnus, tell us, do you like the script?'

'It's all right, but it needs some work on it. Some of the dialogue in the love scenes is a little unnatural.'

'I agree,' said Marta enthusiastically. 'But we can work on that together, you and I.'

Helen didn't stay to hear any more of the conversation, even though she was secretly fascinated, but she wanted to be alone, so after picking up a mug of coffee for herself and taking a couple of biscuits, she excused herself, thinking with some amusement that the others were so engrossed in discussing the art of film making that they hardly noticed her, and leaving the lounge she went upstairs to the bedroom.

Standing at the window, she stared out at the sunlit sea, the red rocks and the ribbed yellow sand of the beach curving about the bay, wishing she could have gone outside, wishing that she had clothes to wear. In this dressing gown of Magnus's she was trapped indoors, his prisoner.

Looking down, she traced the letter embroidered on the breast pocket. M.S. Magnus Scott. Now she knew why he seemed familiar to her. She had seen him on the T.V. screen and she had seen him in a film, but she hadn't remembered his name for some reason. She wasn't much of a filmgoer or a television watcher, but now that she thought about it she had enjoyed the series Marta had referred to, and she had also enjoyed the film she had seen Magnus acting in, and the reason why she had enjoyed both had been him; his presence on the screen, his ability to portray a character, his use of his voice.

He had changed his voice to impersonate Blair and to entice her to this place, and knowing now what his profession was she could understand why he had seemed so changeable yesterday. He had been playing different roles. In turn he had been Blair, then a softly spoken somewhat wild islander, then a cool man of the world who had admitted to deliberately interfering and separating her from Blair to help his friend Wanda Murray.

And lastly, much more recently, he had played

the part of a lover. Helen's hand shook suddenly as she raised the coffee mug to her lips and coffee slopped down the front of the dressing gown. Tears starting in her eyes, she rubbed at the brown stain ineffectually, wondering miserably if Magnus had been acting a part when he had made love to her that morning.

Putting the coffee mug down on the bedside table, she sat down on the edge of the unmade bed, tears streaming down her face. Nothing in her hitherto smooth, unemotional life had prepared her for what had happened downstairs in the lounge, for that emotionally and physically devastating eruption of passion and the need she had felt to be as close as possible to Magnus, to be a part of him. But while it had been happening she had really been convinced that she loved him and that he loved her.

Now the madness of those moments was over and she was able to look back at what had happened more coolly and dispassionately, and to realise how close to performing the act of love they had been. The word act pounded through her head, mocking her. Magnus was an actor, skilled in dissembling, in appearing to be what he wasn't and in pretending to be in love. Had he been pretending he had fallen in love with her when he had kissed and fondled her and had deliberately aroused her until she hadn't cared what else he had done to her?

Covering her face with her hands, she keeled over on to her side and wept as she had never wept before, crying for her lost innocence, crying because never again would she be cool collected Helen Melrose in command of her emotions, in control of her life and knowing exactly where she

was going; crying because she had fallen in love—
at last—but with a man she wasn't sure existed.

Gradually she grew quieter and lay in a sort of
stupor induced by the purging of her emotions, her
mind numb, her limbs lethargic. Warmed by the
mid-morning sun, the room was quiet save for the
sound of waves tumbling on the shore. The steady
murmur of the sea had a soporific effect on Helen.
Her swollen reddened eyelids drooped and she
slipped into the healing oblivion of sleep.

CHAPTER FOUR

EMOTIONALLY and physically drained by the events of the morning, Helen slept for nearly four hours, and when she woke up the room was no longer full of sunlight but was dim, the sun having moved round to the west and away from the sea-facing window. Her head still buried in the pillow, she lay for a few moments in silence, listening. Someone was in the room. She could hear someone breathing. Slowly she turned her head. Magnus was sitting on the side of the bed looking at her, his face devoid of all expression, his blue eyes blank.

A puppet man waiting for the strings to be pulled, she thought rather hysterically, as she remembered she had found out he was an actor. As she sat up she was shaken by a long sobbing shudder. Curling her legs beneath her, she shifted away from him, hunching up against the headboard, staring at him with wide troubled eyes.

'What's wrong, Eilidh?' he demanded roughly. 'Ah, don't look at me like that! I'm not going to hurt you. It was never my intention to hurt you.'

She pushed a long swathe of her hair behind one ear and taking a deep breath tried to control the feeling of revulsion which was shivering through her. Licking her dry lips, she whispered,

'I know your last name now. It . . . it's Scott.'

'How? How do you know?' he demanded, frowning at her.

'Marta Nielsen told me.'

'I see.' His lips twisted wryly. 'So? Does knowing my name make a difference?'

'I know also that you're an actor . . . and where I've seen you before. I saw you acting in a series on television and once in a film. It was a spy story . . . about the last war.'

'That's where I guessed you'd seen me,' he muttered, then added rather viciously, 'Well, I wish they hadn't come. I wish they hadn't seen you here with me.'

'Why didn't you tell me your name and where I might have seen you?' she asked.

'I don't know.' He glanced away from her and then rising to his feet walked away from her, over to the window. Against the bright panes of glass through which the sky, still blue, still bright with sunlight, could be seen, his figure was a dark shape, the shoulders set straight, the head with its ruffled hair held high. After a while he said in a low voice,

'No, that's a lie. I do know why I didn't tell you.' He swung round to face her, but because his back was to the light it was difficult for her to see his face. 'I didn't want you to know my name or what I did for a living because I didn't want you blabbing to everyone that you'd spent the weekend with the film actor Magnus Scott on the island of Carroch when you returned to your work on Tuesday morning,' he said, bitterness grating in his voice. 'I've had that happen to me before . . . not here, but when I was filming in Hollywood, and it caused me nothing but trouble.'

'I wouldn't have blabbed,' Helen retorted, her head going up. She looked at him disdainfully from under her lashes. 'I never blab. Anyway, why would I want to tell anyone about spending a weekend with you?' she continued scornfully. 'What's so wonderful about spending three days on a remote island with a man you can't be sure of and who's pretending all the time? Oh, I wouldn't have told anyone about you or about being here with you, you can be sure of that. You and being with you are nothing to write home about,' she finished bitingly.

There was a tense little silence as they glared at each other across the space which separated them, then Magnus laughed heartily, his head going back, his teeth flashing. Still chuckling, he came towards the bed and sat down again. Leaning towards her, he took hold of both her hands in his, and immediately she was aware of his warmth and strength, of the exciting male scents of his skin and hair.

'You're very good for me, Eilidh,' he said softly. 'You know just how to prick the oversized balloon of my ego.'

'Is it oversized, your ego?' she murmured, suddenly shy again, avoiding the dense blueness of his eyes, looking down at their joined hands.

'Oh, yes. It always has been. Ask anyone who knows me well. Ask Wanda. Ask Blair. Ask my mother,' he said, the bitterness back in his voice. 'All right, so I accept what you say, that you wouldn't have talked indiscreetly about being here with me, but I still wish you hadn't been seen here with me by Max Fiedler.'

She glanced up at him. He was frowning and still looking at her, and once again she had the feeling that he was a friend, a friend who cared about her. In the next instant she was rejecting the feeling, reminding herself that he could be acting.

She withdrew her hands from his, not because she didn't like having hers held by that vital grasp, but because she felt safer when he wasn't touching her, more in control of her feelings.

'Why?' she asked coolly. 'Did he say something to you about me being here?'

'Oh yes, he said a lot—too darn much, and none of it suitable for your ears,' Magnus remarked tautly. He looked right at her, the expression in his eyes frank and steady. 'He assumes you're my latest mistress.'

'Oh!' gasped Helen weakly, and leaned back against the headboard of the bed, her eyelids drooping down quickly to hide her eyes from his direct searching stare, trying to hide from him the sudden turbulence which swirled through her at the thought of being his mistress. 'Am I?' she asked cautiously, giving him a wary look from under her lashes.

'I think you'll agree we hadn't got as far as establishing any relationship between us, before Max arrived,' he said, still dry. 'But just finding you here, dressed in my robe, was enough for him and nothing I could say would change his mind.'

'But does it matter what he thinks,' said Helen, 'if we both know it isn't true?'

'I'm afraid it does. You see, he isn't above using what he saw here for publicity purposes when he announces to the press that he's producing a new film with Rossi directing.' Magnus laughed a little drearily this time, half turning away from her to hold his head in his hands, his elbows resting on his knee. 'In fact he told me exactly what would be in the press release,' he told her.

'Then please will you tell me?' she whispered.

'Why do you want to know?' he asked.

'So that I can determine whether it's really harmful to me.'

'All right. The announcement will of course mention the names of the leading actors in the film, in this case Marta Nielsen and myself. Under both our names there will be a short résumé of our careers to date, what films we've been seen in, and as always there will be something personal—the public who read about such things are always interested in the personal life of actresses and actors, unfortunately,' he said bitterly. 'Marta's two disastrous marriages will be mentioned, as will the name of her latest lover, who happens to be Bill Constantine, the cameraman who works for Fiedler Productions.' His lips twisted in self-mockery. 'And about me,' he continued, 'there will be a reference to my various affairs with different actresses and a mention of the fact that I've recently been staying in a castle on the west coast of Scotland with a female companion called Helen.'

'That's all?' she whispered.

'Isn't it enough?'

'But who will know it's me if my last name isn't mentioned?' she queried.

'Blair will know,' he said quietly, looking at her steadily. 'Wanda will know. And you can be sure neither of them will keep the information to themselves.'

She stared at him in puzzlement, absorbing what he had said and trying to make sense of it.

'You mean ... that you didn't tell Wanda that you would kidnap ... I mean entice me to come here?' she queried.

'No. I just said when she asked me if I could think up a way of preventing you and Blair from going away together this weekend that I'd see what I could do.' He paused again and frowned at the floor. 'You see, Eilidh, we thought, Wanda and I—we thought you'd be different from what you are.'

'Oh, what did you think I'd be like?' she asked in surprise.

'We thought you'd be a hard-faced sex kitten on the make, looking forward to having a flighty weekend in the country with a man who'd taken your fancy,' he said dryly, and turned to her again, looking at her with darkened, troubled eyes. 'I certainly didn't imagine you'd be like you are, innocent and shy. I'm sorry, Eilidh. I made a mistake and did the wrong thing in bringing you here and in making you stay, and all I can think of to make amends is to take you to the mainland now; take you to Blair and explain to him that it wasn't your fault you didn't meet him yesterday afternoon and tell him he isn't to believe anything he might read or hear about you in connection with me.'

'But ... but my clothes? What will I wear?' she exclaimed, thinking practically, in an attempt to ignore the disappointment that swelled up in her suddenly. Magnus didn't really want her after all, and what had happened between them had all been an act on his part; a pretence of loving.

'*Damn!*' he swore, thrusting his fingers through his hair. 'I'd forgotten about that. They're at the bottom of the strait, aren't they?'

'Yes. And the others, the ones I was wearing, won't be dry yet.'

'There must be some here ... some women's clothes, I mean, that will fit you,' he said, rising to his feet again. 'I'm sure Wanda will have left some.'

'Wanda? Wanda Murray?' Helen exclaimed sharply. 'She's been here? She's stayed here with you?'

'She's stayed here, yes,' he replied. 'Several times. She was here last week. That was when she asked me to help her to get you away from Blair for a while. Come with me, upstairs to her bedroom, and see for yourself if there's anything that will fit you.'

He was stepping through the doorway before she could think up a protest, and reluctantly she slid off the bed, and tightening the belt to the robe about her waist she followed him, climbing up the second flight of stairs.

Wanda's bedroom was directly above the one Helen had slept in. From its windows there were panoramic views of the other islands as well as the green hills of Kintyre. It was comfortably furnished with a fourposter bed, an antique dressing table and a wardrobe. The predominant colours in the curtains and bed coverings were yellow and orange and a thick yellow carpet covered the floor.

To Helen's surprise there were many personal objects scattered about the room, and in particular her attention was drawn by some framed photographs arranged on the wall. One was of a middle-aged couple standing with a young woman whom she recognised, from the cloud of red-gold hair and deep blue eyes, as Wanda Murray. A rather ancient, much worn teddy-bear sat on the pillow at the top of the bed and there was a silver-backed brush and comb set on the dressing table. It looked as if Wanda Murray was a frequent visitor to the castle.

Magnus swung open the wardrobe door. A few clothes, mostly casual tweed pants, jeans, shirts and sweaters, hung on hangers. He gestured towards them.

'Take your pick,' he said. 'I'm sure Wanda won't mind.' He turned to one of the chests of drawers and pulled open a drawer. 'And there are some underclothes too.' He turned back to her. 'I'll leave you to change and go and change myself. It's quite a long way to the Trossachs from here. In fact if I'd wanted to go to Callander I wouldn't start from here.'

'Callander?' Helen exclaimed.

'That's right. That's where Blair would probably have taken you for the weekend. His family have a country house there. But I'll phone before we set out, from the Macleishes' cottage, to make sure Wanda and he are still there.'

'Magnus, it really isn't necessary for you to take me to see them. I . . . I can explain to Blair what happened when I see him on Tuesday at the hospital,' Helen said urgently.

'No, I think I should do the explaining,' he replied firmly. 'I made the mistake, got you into this mess, so I'll get you out of it. If they're still at Callander we'll go to Callander today. If they're not, if Blair has returned to Glencross, we'll go there. I have to do this, Helen, to clear my conscience where you're concerned, so bear with me.'

He went from the room, and with a sigh Helen went over to the wardrobe. How everything had changed in a few hours! This morning when she had pleaded with Magnus to take her to the mainland he had refused adamantly. Now, when she did not want to go, when she would have preferred to have stayed tonight and tomorrow and the next day, he insisted that she should leave with him.

From the clothes in the wardrobe she chose a pair of jeans, a cotton shirt and a Fair Isle sweater, all of which looked as if they would fit her, and from the chest of drawers she borrowed a bra and some panties. When she was dressed she combed her hair with the silver-backed comb and tied it back with a piece of ribbon she found in a box of odds and ends on the dressing table. Then she studied the photographs more closely, discovering that there was one of Blair. But then there was also one of Magnus.

'Ready?' Magnus spoke from the doorway. He had changed from jeans into well cut dark pants, a white silk shirt, open at the neck, and a belted jacket of dark blue suede.

'Is Wanda your mistress?' The words were blurted out before Helen could bite them back. They were an expression of what was uppermost in her mind and had been ever since Marta Nielsen had told her of Max Fiedler's suspicions concerning Magnus and Wanda.

'Not bloody likely,' retorted Magnus with a grin. 'Even if she wasn't my half-sister I wouldn't like to live with her.'

'Wanda is your half-sister?' Helen repeated in amazement.

'She is. We have the same mother.' His grin softened into an affectionate smile as he looked at the photograph of the middle-aged couple. 'There she is, dear old Mum, Megan Scott. You may have heard of her too, and seen her. She's a singer too, a concert singer. You may have heard her on recordings of Handel's *Messiah*, or if you like listening to classical music you may have heard her performance of Schubert and Brahm's *lieder*.'

Helen stared at the photograph, at the plump smiling woman with the deep blue eyes and the white wavy hair. Oh, yes, she recognised Megan Scott all right, the Scottish soprano with the sweet yet strong voice who had made an international reputation for herself as a singer. Her glance slid from the woman to the man standing beside her. He was also smiling, a broad-faced stockily built man dressed in tweeds.

'And the man? Who is he?' she asked.

'Wanda's father, Alec Murray. Do you feel better now that you've straightened out the relationships?' Magnus mocked her lightly.

'Yes. You see, I was puzzled. Marta Nielsen said that Max Fiedler suspected that you were going to marry Wanda Murray because you're often in her company, and—well, I just couldn't fit it in with what you did yesterday to separate me from Blair so that Wanda could have him to herself.' She glanced around the room. 'Marta also said she envied you the possession of this castle. Does it really belong to you?'

'It actually belongs to my mother. Her father left it to her when he died a few years ago. But even before then Wanda and I used to come here often. We've both used it as a place to get away from it all; a place where we can both be ourselves instead of what the public want us to be and, believe me, that's very necessary when you're an entertainer and spend a lot of your time in the full glare of publicity.' His face tightened grimly and he turned away to the door. 'Let's go now.'

'What shall I do with your robe?' she asked.

'Give it to me. I'll throw it into my room.'

Harlequin Presents...
VIOLET WINSPEAR
time of the temptress

Harlequin Presents...
SALLY WENTWORTH
say hello to yesterday

Harlequin Presents...
CHARLOTTE LAMB
man's world

Harlequin Presents...
ANNE MATHER
born out of love

Say Hello to Yesterday
Holly Weston had done it all alone.

She had raised her small son and worked her way up to features writer for a major newspaper. Still the bitterness of the the past seven years lingered.

She had been very young when she married Nick Falconer—but old enough to lose her heart completely when he left. Despite her success in her new life, her old one haunted her.

But it was over and done with—until an assignment in Greece brought her face to face with Nick, and all she was trying to forget. . . .

Time of the Temptress
The game must be played his way!

Rebellion against a cushioned, controlled life had landed Eve Tarrant in Africa. Now only the tough mercenary Wade O'Mara stood between her and possible death in the wild, revolution-torn jungle.

But the real danger was Wade himself—he had made Eve aware of herself as a woman.

"I saved your neck, so you feel you owe me something," Wade said. "But you don't owe me a thing, Eve. Get away from me." She knew she could make him lose his head if she tried. But that wouldn't solve anything. . . .

Your Romantic Adventure Starts Here.

Born Out of Love
It had to be coincidence!

Charlotte stared at the man through a mist of confusion. It was Logan, of course, but unmistakably the man who had ravaged her emotions and then abandoned her all those years ago.

She ought to feel angry. She ought to feel resentful and cheated. Instead, she was apprehensive—terrified at the complications he could create.

"We are not through, Charlotte," he told her flatly. "I sometimes think we haven't even begun."

Man's World
Kate was finished with love for good.

Kate's new boss, features editor Eliot Holman, might have devastating charms—but Kate couldn't care less, even if it was obvious that he was interested in her.

Everyone, including Eliot, though Kate was grieving over the loss of her husband, Toby. She kept it a carefully guarded secret just how cruelly Toby had treated her and how terrified she was of trusting men again.

But Eliot refused to leave her alone, which only served to infuriate her. He was no different from any other man. . . or was he?

He went ahead of her along the landing, pausing at the doorway of another room to toss the robe inside before running down the stairs.

'Do you think I could have something to eat before we leave?' Helen asked, following him into the kitchen and thinking it was a way to delay their departure. Perhaps if she could delay it even an hour he might decide then it was too late to set off for Callander and would postpone it until tomorrow.

Surprised and a little amused at her own deviousness, she waited for his answer. It came in a way she hadn't expected. From behind her his hands slid over her shoulders down over her breasts and she was pulled back against him. When he bent his head his cheek brushed against hers.

'You know, I'm fast getting the impression that contrary to what you said this morning you don't want to leave Carroch,' he whispered, and turning his head he nibbled her ear lobe. The light slightly mocking caress sent all sorts of delicious tingles shooting along her nerves, and pivoting on her feet, which were still bare because she hadn't found anything to put on them in Wanda's room, she turned within the circle of his arms to face him. 'Would I be right?' he queried.

'Yes, you would be right,' she replied shyly, putting her arms around his neck and hiding her face in the silkiness of his shirt. 'But it isn't Carroch I don't want to leave,' she added softly.

Magnus didn't say anything but his arms tightened about her and his hands slid over her back caressingly. After a few moments he straightened up and putting his hands on her shoulders pushed her away from him, but still held her shoulders while he looked down at her, his eyes searching her face. She looked back at him serenely.

'Eilidh, please try to understand,' he said huskily. 'I can't let you stay here with me any longer.'

'Why not?'

'I . . .' He broke off, his hands dropping away from her abruptly. Thrusting them into his jacket pockets, he stared down at his feet, his face set in stern lines. 'I don't trust myself,' he said gratingly. 'I don't trust myself not to make love to you, if we stay. Remember what nearly happened this morning, what would have happened if Max and the other two hadn't turned up.'

'Yes, I remember,' she whispered.

'Then come on, let's go to the boat and cross over to Macleish's cottage and phone Blair and Wanda,' he said autocratically, marching towards the porch and opening the door.

'I can't. I can't come. I haven't any shoes. Wanda's shoes don't fit me and my own . . . well, look at them!' Helen picked up her shoes from where she had put them. They were still sodden with sea-water, their shape distorted.

'There's a pair of seaboots out here that might fit you,' Magnus replied, his voice muffled as he bent down in the porch. When he straightened up he flung the seaboots into the kitchen and staying in the porch proceeded to pull on his own boots.

Reluctantly Helen picked up the seaboots and stepped into them. They were cool and clammy and just a little too long, but she could walk in them.

'Okay?' queried Magnus, looking in from the porch. He was slipping the yellow waterproof jacket on over his suede jacket. 'There's one of these you can wear too. It's Wanda's.'

Holding the yellow jacket in his hand, he stepped back into the kitchen towards her. Helen put a hand to her head and swayed slightly. Backing away from him, she leaned a hand on the table as if for support and moaned.

'Oh, I'm so hungry,' she said gaspingly. 'I'm starving! I haven't had anything to eat since breakfast, and I can't possibly go on a journey without eating something now. If I don't eat soon I'll . . . I'll faint. Oh, I think I'm going to faint now!'

'*Damn!*' The oath crisped from his throat. 'Women!' he added scathingly, and dropped the waterproof to the floor. Stepping over to her, he seized her by the shoulders and pushed her down on one of the chairs. 'Now what would you like to eat?' he asked.

With one hand shielding her eyes and part of her face in case he saw that she was nearly laughing and not at all near to fainting, Helen whispered,

'I'd like a good dinner. I haven't really had anything decent to eat since I came here.'

'I cooked a meal for you last night,' he exclaimed. 'And I told you to help yourself if you wanted anything. You could have had some lunch with Marta, me and the others if you'd wanted instead of hiding away in the bedroom. You've only yourself to blame if you're hungry.'

'Oh, you're not very nice,' Helen retorted, abandoning her pretence at feeling faint because it didn't seem to be having the right effect on him. He wasn't at all concerned about her wellbeing now.

'No, I'm not,' he agreed tautly. 'As I tried to tell you last night.' He was eyeing her cynically. 'And you can stop putting on an act. You're nowhere near fainting!' Swinging away from her, he went over to the refrigerator, opened the door and took out a jug of milk. 'You can have some milk and I'll make you a ham sandwich,' he said crisply. 'We'll stop somewhere on the way to Callander for a meal at a hotel.'

'But I don't want to go to Callander. And I don't want to see Blair or Wanda,' she protested.

'Funny how you've changed your mind since you've found out who I am, isn't it?' he sneered.

'It has nothing to do with who or what you are,' Helen retorted furiously. 'I'm not leaving here until I've had a decent meal, and there's nothing you can do to make me leave until I'm ready to go!'

Kicking off the rubber boots, she walked out of the kitchen and up the stairs to her bedroom, her lips curving wryly as she looked around the room. She was certainly spending a lot of time in it and she was glad it was comfortable. Going over to the bed, she began to straighten it, plumping the pillows, smoothing the sheets and putting the cover in place. Then carrying the small armchair over to the window, she sat down in it and looked out at the view. She would wait for a while and if Magnus didn't come up to try and persuade her to go over to the mainland again she would go downstairs and make a meal for herself.

At the end of half an hour she was feeling fidgety and hungrier than ever, and Magnus hadn't bothered to come up, so she left the bedroom and crept downstairs to the kitchen.

Magnus wasn't there, and she wondered if he had gone outside or whether he was in the lounge. But she wasn't going to look for him, not yet. She was going to cook a meal first—a proper dinner with meat and vegetables, with a dessert to follow. She would cook enough for the two of them and he could have some or not.

She had always taken pleasure in cooking, having been taught by her mother, who was trained in domestic science and was still teaching at a high school near Dumfries, and soon she was completely absorbed in creating a meal from the ingredients which she found in the refrigerator and the cupboards. An hour or so later she was in the dining room, in the process of setting the table with the lace dinner mats and silver cutlery she had found in the sideboard, when she heard Magnus enter the house. For a moment she listened to find out which direction he would move from the kitchen, but heard nothing, so she took some long green candles she had found in a box on the sideboard and put them in the silver candlesticks which decorated the long refectory table. When everything was done to her satisfaction she stood back to admire the table, the shining wood, the glinting silverware, the delicate foam of the lace mats.

'What the hell do you think you're doing?' Magnus spoke from the doorway, and she turned to face him.

'Enjoying myself,' she said serenely. 'You have some lovely tableware. Some of it must be very valuable as antiques.'

'It all belonged to my grandparents,' he replied coolly.

'I've cooked enough dinner for the two of us,'

she went on, 'because I thought you might like
some too.'

'Thank you.' He was still stiff and cool and he
looking at her suspiciously. 'I've been over to the
mainland,' he said abruptly. 'I phoned the Calder
house at Callander from the Macleishes'. There
was no answer, so I phoned Wanda's flat in
London. Her maid said she'd gone away for the
weekend. Then I decided to try Blair's house in
Glencross.' His lips twisted wryly. 'Third time
lucky,' he drawled. 'He was at home and he
answered the phone.'

'What did he say?'

'He thought at first that I was someone from the
local police station calling in with news about you.
It seems that when you weren't at your flat
yesterday, when he went there to pick you up, he
started to look for you. He tried the hospital first
and then he phoned your parents.'

'Oh, no!' gasped Helen.

'They, of course, knew nothing of your
whereabouts, but when he couldn't locate you
Blair phoned them again the next day and asked
their permission to inform the police that you were
missing and to ask them to look out for you and
your car in case you'd had an accident somewhere.'
Magnus's expression was sardonic. 'He's been in
one heck of a tizzy and has stayed near the phone
all yesterday, all last night and all today, waiting
to hear from you or of you.'

'But Wanda? What about Wanda?' exclaimed
Helen. 'Isn't she with him?'

'Oh, she turned up at his house just as she'd
planned, but he refused to go away with her and
this morning they had a row and she left the house
in a huff.' Magnus ruffled his hair, sighed and

looked suddenly weary and disillusioned. 'God knows if she'll go back now,' he said. 'I might as well have not bothered to help her.' A wintry smile tugged at the corners of his mouth. 'As Rabbie Burns wrote: *"The best laid schemes o' mice and men gang aft agley,"* and my scheme to help Wanda seems to be very *agley*.' With a shrug he turned away and walked across the hall into the lounge.

After a moment Helen followed him. He was in the process of pouring a generous measure of whisky into a glass.

'Did you tell Blair what happened yesterday and why I wasn't at my flat when he went there to pick me up?' she asked.

'No. I thought it best not to mention that I know anything about you.' He put the decanter down, drank most of the liquor in the glass at one gulp, and shook his head afterwards against the jolt of the raw spirit. 'Especially since he's asked the police to keep a lookout for you.' He gave her a glance which glittered now with hostility and poured more whisky into the glass. 'If I'd told him he would probably have accused me of kidnapping you and before we could do anything about it he'd have told the press. And that's the sort of publicity I can do without.' He gave her another sour look. 'And now I'm beginning to wish I'd never heard of you and that I'd never tried to help Wanda. I should have known better. It's not the first time I've rushed in where an angel would fear to tread, just to help her out of the messes she's got herself into by her own erratic behaviour. *Women!*' he added scathingly.

'I'm sorry,' muttered Helen out of the turmoil of her thoughts, although she wasn't quite sure what she was apologising for. Why should she apologise to Magnus? He was to blame for the whole situation. If he hadn't been such a quixotic fool thinking he could help Wanda to save her marriage by preventing another woman from going away with Blair, Blair wouldn't be thinking she'd been abducted and he wouldn't have asked the police to look out for her, and. . . .

And she wouldn't have ever met Magnus and been drawn into the magnetic field of his personality. She wouldn't have met him and fallen in love with him to such an extent that her own behaviour had undergone a transformation in a matter of a few hours, and now she didn't want to leave him and go back to Glencross. Most of all she didn't want to have anything to do with Blair any more.

'Excuse me, I think something might be burning,' she muttered, and hurried back to the kitchen. She was just in time to prevent the vegetables from catching on the bottom of the pan they were in, and for the next fifteen minutes she was too busy attending to the cooking to spare time for anything else and when she went back to the lounge the lamps were on to disperse the dimness which had crept into the room now that the sun was right round to the north-west and about to set so that the south-facing side of the castle was in the shadow.

Magnus was sitting at the desk. His jacket was off, his hair was in wild disorder and he was staring morosely at the thick sheaf of papers he had been reading the previous night and which Helen now guessed was the script for the film Max Fiedler and Leo Rossi wanted him to act in. Before him was the decanter and the glass which had been recently refilled with whisky.

'Dinner is ready if you'd like to have some,' she said. 'I've roasted the sirloin of beef I found in the fridge, and there's roast potatoes and Yorkshire pudding to go with it. I've also made a lemon pudding.'

Magnus gave her a sidelong glance from under fiercely frowning black eyebrows.

'I wish I knew what you're up to,' he growled at her. 'Did someone once tell you that the surest way to a man's heart is through his stomach?'

'I'm not up to anything,' she retorted. 'I just think we should both have a decent meal.' She directed a scornful glance at the empty decanter. 'You might be able to operate on an empty stomach or when you're full of neat Scotch, but I can't. I have to have three meals a day, regularly, or . . . or I stop behaving sensibly.' Turning on her heel, she walked back to the doorway. 'I'm going to dish the food up now. Shall I put some out for you?' she asked, pausing but not looking back at him.

'If you must,' was the ungracious answer. 'I wouldn't like you to feel all your efforts to cook were wasted.'

She swung round then to glare at him, encountered a disturbingly mocking glance from brilliant blue eyes and turned away quickly to hurry back to the kitchen.

When she carried a tray with two plates filled with meat, vegetables and Yorkshire pudding through into the dining room, Magnus was already there, sitting at the head of the table in the beautiful carved Jacobean chair, in the process of pouring red wine into two glasses. Helen placed a plate in front of him and put her own down in the other place she had set, which was on the side of the table, just to the right of his. Then she sat down on the long bench. The candles, which he must have lit, burned steadily, the light from their flames gleaming on polished oak and shiny silver, creating a golden glow in the middle of the dark room, giving everything a soft, rich look.

'I didn't know there was any wine,' Helen remarked.

'Of course you didn't,' he retorted. In the candlelight his eyes were indigo, dark and mysterious. 'I always have a few bottles handy just in case I have a woman guest. It goes with a candlelit dinner, don't you agree? A very necessary preliminary to seduction.'

A strong tingle of excitement danced along Helen's nerves and she looked down quickly at her plate. Picking up her knife and fork, she began to eat, giving the impression that she was not at all impressed by the challenge implicit in his mocking remarks or that she hadn't understood it, and for a while there was silence, as, both of them being ravenous, they ate the perfectly cooked delicious food.

'That was very good,' Magnus announced, finishing before she did and pouring more wine into his empty glass.

'Would you like some more?' asked Helen politely.

'Yes, but I'll get it,' he said, rising to his feet. He left the room with his empty plate, returning with it piled with more meat and vegetables. 'I've left some for you,' he said as he sat down. 'You haven't drunk much of your wine. Don't you like it?'

'Yes, but I'm not very used to wine. I drink it rarely.'

'Only when you dine tête-à-tête, cosily with Blair, I suppose,' he sneered. 'Do you often cook for him like this?'

'Not often. A couple of times only,' she replied.

'But enough to show him what a good wife you'd be if only he were free to marry you,' he continued jeeringly. 'Oh, yes, I'm beginning to realise Wanda has left her move to get Blair back too late. She can't possibly compete with you. She can't cook and never has. Nor can she keep house. Singing and entertaining are all she likes to do. Being the supportive do-everything wife has never been in her line.'

'Then why did she marry Blair?' Helen demanded. 'If she didn't want to carry out the promises she made when they were married why did she go through with the ceremony?'

Leaning back in his chair, Magnus raised his wine glass to his lips and sipped, looking at her all the time, his eyes glinting with mockery.

'Can't you guess?' he remarked, with a cynical twist to his lips. 'They met, fell in love, fell into bed together, and three months later she discovered she was going to have his child. She wanted the birth to be legal, so she coaxed Blair into marrying her.'

'Oh, I didn't know,' muttered Helen, suddenly flustered. Picking up her wine glass, she drank some of the smooth but rather heavy burgundy. 'I didn't know there was a child—Blair has never said anything about him.'

'*Her*. Ailsa is nearly eleven now.'

'Does she live with Wanda?'

'Only when she isn't at boarding school. I believe she does spend some time with Blair, in the summer, at the house in Callander.'

'How awful for her, being shunted from one parent to another,' sighed Helen.

'Now, save your sympathy for someone who really needs it,' Magnus cautioned her softly. 'Ailsa doesn't need it. She's a tough child, quite able to hold her own in this world. And it's better that she should live the way she does than to be living with two parents who are always fighting.' He picked up the wine bottle and tipped it over her almost empty glass. 'But I can see I'm shocking your romantic idealism,' he remarked dryly. 'You believe in marriage, don't you?'

'Yes, I do. Why shouldn't I? My own parents have been happily married for over twenty-five years and so have many of their friends and acquaintances, so it's easy for me to believe marriage can be successful. It doesn't have to fail, not if the partners love each other—I mean really love each other and are willing to give as well as take, don't bear grudges and truly trust each other.' She noticed he was looking cynical again and added defiantly, 'Oh, I don't expect you to understand. The sort of people you work with are changing partners all the time. Why, even your own mother. . . .' She broke off, realising that she was about to make a prejudiced remark about his mother, and rose to her feet. 'I'm sorry,' she said stiffly, picking up their empty plates. 'I've no right to pass judgment on your mother when I don't know her. I'll go and fetch the pudding.'

When she returned to the dining room Magnus was still sitting where she had left him, fiddling with his wineglass, scowling down at the wine in it. He moved back so she could put the dish of pudding in front of him and watched her sit down at the table.

'My mother would like you, Eilidh,' he said quietly. 'She would like your no-nonsense attitude to life and your belief that love is the basis of all good marriages, because that's her belief too.' He picked up his dessert spoon and scooped up some pudding. 'She and *my* father were never married.'

'Oh,' said Helen, inadequately, and ate some pudding. Smooth and creamy, delicately flavoured with lemon juice and rind, it melted in the mouth. 'Why not?' she asked, curiosity getting the better of her.

'They intended to, apparently, but he was killed in an accident when he was making a film in Hollywood just before he was supposed to come here to marry her in Scotland.' His mouth quirked wryly. 'They'd anticipated the ceremony by a few weeks, although my mother didn't know she was expecting me until a couple of months after his death. That's why I use her name—her maiden name.'

'Your father was an actor too?'

'Yes. He was just making his name in films when he was killed.'

'British?'

'No. He was an American, from New York. Mmm, this is very good pudding, Eilidh.' He slanted her a glance of pure mockery. 'If you were to stay here much longer and cook meals like this I would really make you my prisoner and never, never let you go.'

'How . . . how could you do that? Keep me prisoner, I mean,' she challenged. The wine she had drunk was singing a little in her head, making her reckless.

'I'd make love to you all the time, except when

you had to cook, of course. We'd live on kisses and lemon pudding,' he replied lightly.

Helen laughed, delighted by such nonsense, and then was immediately overwhelmed by regret because it could never be. She would never be the prisoner of his love, because if he wanted her to be his possession he would have to become her possession, and she was quite sure he would never agree to such terms. He would never agree to marry her because he valued his freedom too highly.

She sighed, unaware that she did, and let her spoon drop into her dish. She had eaten only a third of her helping of pudding, but suddenly she had no appetite for more.

'What's the matter, Eilidh? What's making you sigh?' Magnus leaned across the corner of the table and covered her left hand which was lying beside her dish with his own right hand. The long fingers curled about hers comfortingly and once again she had the impression that he was her friend, that he was really concerned about her and wanted to help her.

'I wish Blair hadn't told my parents that he couldn't find me. They'll be quite worried,' she muttered, which wasn't what she was wishing at all. 'I wish you'd told him that I'm here with you and asked him to tell the police to stop looking for me.'

Gently his thumb stroked the delicate skin on the underside of her wrist. No one had ever done that to her before, and she was surprised by the exquisite sensations that such a slight caress could arouse.

'We'll go over, then, and you can phone him from the Macleishes' house to tell him you're on your way back to Glencross,' he said softly.

'But I don't want to. . . .' she began, her voice barely audible, her cheeks burning suddenly as she faced up to the reality of her desire to stay with him, to lie close to him as she had that morning in the lounge and to feel again passion throbbing through him and herself expanding, opening and welcoming him. She pulled her hand from under his and stood up. 'It doesn't matter,' she said stiffly. 'I'll go and make some coffee.'

In the kitchen, her nerves twanging with frustration because she hadn't been able to say to him what she really wished, she put on the kettle and set out coffee cups. She was secretly amazed all the time by her own behaviour when she was with him, the way she seesawed between aggressiveness and prudish shyness. Magnus was really dangerous for her to know, because he could change her from what she had been before she had met him, from a cool, almost sexless person into a woman overflowing with sensual desires. How shocked her parents would be if they knew that when she was with Magnus she wanted to go to bed with him and make love with him, even though she had known him only about thirty hours, that she was bewitched by a man who wasn't interested in marriage and who was known for the affairs he had had with various film actresses.

Her parents! They must be wondering where she was. How foolishly she had behaved! She should have gone with Magnus to the mainland when he had wanted to take her. If she had gone with him she would have been part way to Glencross by now and neither Blair nor her parents need have known where she had been or with whom she had been during the past day and night.

She looked at the kitchen clock. Nine-thirty. The sun was setting and behind the curve of the moorland which she could see through the window the sky was a pale duck-egg green streaked with crimson and gold clouds. There was still time to go over to the mainland as Magnus had suggested and ask Archie Macleish to start her car.

Picking up the tray, she carried it into the dining room. Magnus wasn't there and the candles were guttering, the tops of them melting away, wax running down their sides. Deciding he must have gone to sit in the lounge, Helen extinguished the candles with the antique silver extinguisher and carried the tray into the other room.

He wasn't there either, so she set the tray down on the coffee table and sitting on the sofa poured coffee into the two cups, assuming he would come into the room eventually. Half an hour later the shadows in the corners of the room where the lamplight didn't reach were deep and purple, she was still sitting on the sofa and Magnus had not come. The coffee in the pot and the cups was cold.

CHAPTER FIVE

HELEN became aware that she was sitting tensely on the edge of the sofa and listening to the silence of the castle; listening for sounds of Magnus moving about. Where was he? Had he gone out again? If he had he must have left by the front door, because he hadn't come through the kitchen to the back door while she had been making the coffee. She glanced at the window. It was dark outside now. Was it too late to ask him to take her to the mainland? Would he be willing to cross the strait in the dark? The only way to find out was to ask him. But where was he?

Picking up the tray, she carried it out to the kitchen and from force of habit washed up and put everything away and, after making sure that the kitchen was as clean and tidy as she would like to find it after someone else had cooked in it, she went upstairs. On the second landing she paused to look in the rooms she had used, the bathroom and the bedroom at the back of the tower. All were dark and Magnus wasn't in any of them. Switching on another light, she mounted the second flight of stairs and went straight to his room. The door was partially open but there was no light on. She looked into the room. A breeze coming in through an open door which was set into the outer wall of the room stirred the curtains at the window.

Crossing the room to the open door, she looked outside on to the battlements of the tower. Behind

the stone parapet was a narrow wall-walk and she
guessed that Magnus had gone outside, possibly to
view the sunset from such a wonderful viewpoint.
But the sun had set almost forty minutes ago and
the sky was almost completely dark blue now, at
least as dark as it would ever become in that
northern latitude during the summer.

Was Magnus still outside? Curious to find out
how far it was possible to see from the
battlements, Helen stepped out and looked
through one of the gaps in the parapet, one of the
openings through which a defender of the tower in
days gone by would have fired an arrow or even a
gun, shooting downwards on any attacker while
remaining concealed behind the sturdy 'cops' or
'merlons', as the raised parts of the parapet were
called.

Far below, glinting with reflected starlight, the
water in the bay creamed along the narrow beach
and occasionally leapt in flashes of sparkling foam
against jutting rocks. Beyond the entrance to the
bay, right down the Sound, lights twinkled on
indiscernible land from scattered houses on the
island of Jura and the opposite mainland. The
night air was soft and warm, still holding some of
the heat of the sun which had shone all day.

Withdrawing from the gap, Helen walked slowly
along the wall-walk to a small turret with a
pointed slate roof built at the corner of the
battlements and walked through it to the west side
of the tower, thinking she might find Magnus still
there watching the last streaks of light fading in
the sky. But the wall-walk was shadowed and
empty and when she looked through a gap all she
could see was the dark shape of another
mountainous island which loomed beyond the

limits of Carroch, dark blue against the blue-grey of the western sky.

She walked on, stopping on the northern side and on the eastern side to look out, wishing she had thought to come up during the daytime when the views in such clear weather must have been magnificent, and eventually returned to the southern side and the door which opened out of Magnus's bedroom.

The door was shut. Thinking it has been blown shut by the wind, she felt for a knob to open it and found none. She was shut out in the dark in that high windy place, and the only way she could think of to get back inside would be to smash a windowpane—if she could find anything to smash it with—and release the catch on the inside of the window so as to open it, a piece of vandalism from which she retreated, having too much respect for other people's property to damage it.

'Magnus!' she shouted. 'Magnus!' Then she thumped hard on the sturdy wooden door and waited quietly for something to happen. She didn't frighten easily, but there was something creepy about being out on the narrow wall-walk so high above ground level and she didn't fancy spending the night up there. The door didn't open and no light went on in the room, so she banged on the door again, thumping with both fists and shouting for help at the top of her voice. Then, breathless from her efforts, she leaned against the door, feeling panic needle through her as she realised that if Magnus was downstairs he might not hear her and she would have to wait until he came up to bed, if he did come up and didn't stay in the lounge all night drinking whisky.

'Magnus—oh, Magnus!' she cried, and banged again on the door.

Suddenly light slanted out through the window. The door opened abruptly while she was still leaning against it and she fell forward into the lamplit room. She was caught and held steady by Magnus, who grasped her arms above the elbow. He was dressed only in black silk pyjama pants and in the lamplight the suntanned bare skin of his chest, arms and shoulders gleamed like gold. From under puzzled frowning brows his blue eyes stared at her.

'What were you doing out there?' he demanded.

'I was looking for you,' she gasped. 'Oh, I'm so glad you heard me banging on the door! I thought I'd be out there for the night. I made coffee, but when you didn't come to have some I came upstairs to find you. I saw the door open and thought you must be out on the battlements. Were you?'

'No.' He let go of her arms and stepped past her to close the door, then turned to face her. 'While you were making the coffee I went out, the front way, took a walk along the beach.' His sudden grin was slightly crooked and self-mocking. 'It was to clear my head of too much wine on top of too much whisky,' he added wryly. 'When I came back into the house you weren't in the kitchen or anywhere else downstairs, so I decided that you'd gone to bed and thought I might as well get a good night's sleep myself. I came up here, found the door open ... I must have left it open when I was up here this morning, showing Marta and Leo and Max the view. I'd no idea you were up here or I wouldn't have closed it. I was just going to sleep when I heard you shouting and thumping.'

Again his grin mocked himself. 'I didn't open the door at first because I thought I must be imagining things. This tower is supposed to be haunted by a woman, the wife of the Scottish knight who used to own it.' His grin faded and his eyes softened. Stepping towards her, he raised a hand and touched her cheek gently. 'Poor Eilidh,' he murmured. 'You're quite white with fright.'

'I'm all right,' she muttered, stepping back from him as she felt tension sparking between them like an electric shock and sweat sprang on the palms of her hands, making them clammy with the need to touch him. Forgetting that she had been looking for him to ask him to take her to the mainland, she clenched her hands and pushed them into the pockets of Wanda's jeans. 'Thank you for letting me in. I'm sorry I disturbed you. I . . . I think I'll go to bed now—it's getting late. Goodnight.'

She must get away from him before the pull of attraction proved too much for her. She must get out of this warm comfortable room of his and go back to the pleasant but impersonal guest bedroom on the first floor. Turning, she stepped blindly towards the door, only to find he had moved and was standing in her way so that she walked right into him. Once again he grasped her arms to steady her, and immediately she was surrounded by the mysterious masculine scents of his skin and hair and was feeling the heat of his body radiating out to her, encircling her and drawing her close to him.

'Please, Magnus,' she whispered. 'Please let me go.'

'No. You can sleep here, with me,' he replied softly, his hands sliding up her arms to her shoulders and over her back as he impelled her gently, almost imperceptibly towards him.

'I can't—I mustn't,' she muttered half-heartedly, trying to assert mind over matter, trying to control the urge she had to sway towards him, put her arms around him and lift her face for his kiss. 'I . . . I think it would be safer if I didn't stay,' she added.

'Safer for whom? For you? Or for me?'

'For both of us. After tomorrow, after I've left here and gone back to Glencross, we're not likely to see each other again, ever,' she argued, holding herself stiffly so as not to come into contact with him and keeping her head down so that she wouldn't even make eye contact with him.

'Does that mean you're never going to see a film in which I'm acting again?' he asked with a touch of mockery.

'You know that isn't what I meant,' she retorted, still not looking at him. 'I'll go back to Glencross, to my work there in the hospital, and you . . . well, you'll go your way, and the chances of us ever meeting again will be very slim. We'll never meet again, never.'

'You could be right,' he murmured, lifting a hand to her head and undoing the ribbon which held her hair back behind her neck. Shimmering and soft the silken stuff slid over her shoulders and about her cheeks. Magnus tossed the ribbon to the floor and curved his hands about her face under the twin swathes of hair, framing it and lifting it so he could look into her eyes. 'But that isn't a good reason for us not to enjoy each other's company now, while we're still together. Sleep with me, Eilidh, and then neither of us will be lonely tonight. You know you want to. That's really why you didn't want to go to the mainland with me this evening. That's why you came up here looking for me. You want me and I want you—it's as simple as that. In spite of ourselves we're attracted to each other, so why should we back away from each other? Why shouldn't we both have what we want, here and now?'

His voice was deep and persuasive, his eyes were dark, their expression warm and frankly sensual. He was mesmerising her again, using all his skill as a lover to break down her resistance. Against his chest her hands pushed ineffectually, palms and fingers losing their stiffness as soon as they touched him, betraying her.

'Oh, I can't. I mustn't,' she insisted weakly, even while she was caressing him, feeling the roughness of hair and the smoothness of skin, finding a heady delight in touching him so intimately and in hearing his gasp of pleasure as her fingers found and tantalised a particularly sensually vulnerable spot.

'Hey, this isn't fair!' he complained, laughing a little. 'You have me at a disadvantage. To be equal you must take that blouse off. Here, let me help.'

Expertly he undid the fastenings of the blouse and slid the garment from her shoulders, then her head was reeling with the inhaled scents of his hair as it brushed against her face when he lowered his head to kiss the white skin of her shoulders and breast which he had exposed. Her body arched involuntarily against his, her eyes closed and while she was still gasping for breath from the exquisite sensations which were tingling through her Magnus lifted his head and took her lips in a kiss which seemed to scorch right through to the core of her, blasting away the last of her already weak defences.

After that terrible blinding kiss she had no control over what happened next and had no knowledge of how she came to be lying on the bed close to him, the rest of her clothing having been smoothed and stroked away by his eager yet gentle hands.

'You're beautiful, Eilidh,' he murmured, leaning over her while he stroked her slowly and suggestively. 'As sweet and fresh as a daisy, white tipped with gold, and I love you—I love you more than I've ever loved any woman before you. Ah, love me, Eilidh, love me now, tonight, and let the future, all the tomorrows take care of themselves.'

The soft music of his voice lulled her mind while the caresses of his lips and hands were arousing a fiercely passionate response within her body, a desire to please him as he was pleasing her, to love him as he asked to be loved. She didn't like being reminded of those other women he had known and she became suddenly determined to obliterate them from his mind for ever. Moving against him urgently, glorying in the feel of his manhood thrusting against her, she wound her arms about him and kissed his face, his throat everywhere she could in a wild abandonment until, unable to control his own excited passions any longer, he pushed her back against the pillows and the sweet heat of his mouth smothering hers softened the explosive shock of their union.

Pain was sharp but gave way quickly to new sensations which created a turbulence within her that swelled and swelled. Then she seemed to shake and crack apart like the earth shakes and cracks when the wildfire contained within it rises to the surface and bursts forth, and then she was sighing and sagging, laughing and crying all at

once as their bodies melted together and with a
moan of pleasure and satisfaction Magnus buried
his hot face against her throat.

It was the slight chilling of her skin that roused
Helen from the doze induced by satiation into
which she had fallen. She opened her eyes and
looked down. Magnus's head was still resting
against her shoulder and he seemed to be asleep,
one hand lying heavily on her breast and one leg
lying across both of hers as if he sought to keep
her his prisoner even while he slept.

She looked up and across at the oblong grey
which was the window. The night was not yet
over, but she had no idea of actual time. For a
while as they had spun together in the wild
whirlpool of physical passion, time had been of no
account to either of them.

But the moment of loving, the fiery culmination
of passion followed by the sweet fulfilment and
limb-relaxing languor was past. The warm sense of
being united, of being a part of each other, had
gone. Sanity was back, chilling her, separating her
from him, even though he was still lying close to
her.

She glanced down again at the ruffled head, at
the handsome face calm and devoid of expression
in sleep. What had she done? She had done
something she had never done in her life before.
She had lain intimately with this man, yet she
didn't know him. Oh, she knew very well what he
looked like. She knew the thickness of his dark
hair, the deep blue of his eyes, the chiselled
straightness of his bold nose, the beautiful
moulding of his lips. And now, after tonight, she
knew and would remember the feel of his skin
under her hands, the hardness of his thighs

pushing against hers and the tender touch of his
fingertips caressing her.

But she still wasn't sure who he was. She still
felt she hadn't met the real Magnus Scott—or
rather she couldn't tell when he wasn't acting a
part. Even what had happened between them on
this bed, she realised miserably, the wonderful
feeling they had shared of belonging to each other,
could have been an act. . . .

The act of love. The phrase leapt into her mind,
mocking her, and she groaned. Yes, that was what
it had been, for he had said he loved her and she
felt she had loved him, but it wasn't real love, true
love, that they had experienced for each other;
only the urge to satisfy physical desire.

'Oh, what have I done? What have I done?' she
groaned, tears gathering in her eyes and slipping
silently down her cheeks.

Magnus raised his head and looked at her, his
eyelids slanting heavily over the dense blueness of
his eyes. Seeing her tears, he bent to lick them one
by one from her cheeks, then pressed his salt-
tasting lips to hers in another kiss which
threatened to bewitch her again.

'You have made love with me,' he whispered,
when he lifted his lips from hers. He rubbed his
bristly cheek against hers, 'It was good, wasn't it?
As good for you as it was for me?' He raised his
head again to look down at her quizzically, his lips
curving in their half sweet, half mocking smile.

'Yes,' she whispered. 'No.' She twisted her head
from side to side in an agony of confusion. 'Oh,
how can I tell? I've no experience, nothing to
compare it with. I . . . I've never done it before . . .
and now I wish I hadn't. I wish I hadn't!'

His smile faded. His eyebrows frowned, his eyes

lost their warmth and became empty, as expressionless as pieces of blue glass.

'Why?' he demanded. 'Why do you wish that? Are you ashamed of what you've done? Ashamed of being with me, of loving the way we did? Believe me, Eilidh, you have no need to be ashamed. What we did was beautiful and natural.' He paused, his frown deepening as he chewed uncertainly at his lower lip. Then he smiled again as he stroked her hair from the soft white swell of her breast. 'But if you didn't find it satisfactory, we can always try again,' he whispered, his breath fanning her cheek as he bent his head as if to kiss her again.

'No, oh no! It isn't that,' she cried, twisting her head away from the temptation of his lips. 'It's just that I don't know if . . . if you were pretending to . . . to love me or not. You see——' she turned to face him again, feeling safe again because she sensed he had moved away from her. One hand supporting his head, his elbow on the pillow, he was staring at her and frowning again in puzzlement. 'I don't know which is the real you,' she continued in a whisper, and added, her voice cracking a little under the pressure of her agitation, 'I don't know you. I don't know you at all. You're always changing, acting different parts.'

Magnus did not move, but a muscle clenched at his jawline as if he had gritted his teeth and his eyes closed tightly, the heavy lids creasing, the lines radiating out from the upturned corners hardening, and she guessed instinctively that she had hurt him. Then with a quick movement he slid down beside her again and with his eyes open and smiling once more into hers he put his hands on

her arms and brought her close to him, white
and quick-breathing, her tawny eyes wide and
troubled, her kiss-blurred lips drooping a little
sadly.

'All I can say is that I wasn't pretending, Eilidh,
and that you know me as well as I know myself,'
he told her. 'And now let's sleep for another hour
or so. I'd like to leave Carroch as soon as the sun
is up. I've a long way to go tomorrow to be where
I have to be.'

He kissed her again gently and gathered her
against him, stroking her hair soothingly. Calmed
by the tender caress, Helen laid her head on his
chest and soon, warmed by the covers which he
had pulled up and over both of them, she drifted
off to sleep.

He wakened her when the sun was rising and
flooding the room with rosy light, dispersing grey
shadows. He was already dressed in the clothes he
had worn the previous evening, dark pants, white
shirt and blue suede jacket. His hair was damp and
sleek, although one recalcitrant lock was beginning
to slide forward over his forehead and he was
freshly shaved. But there were dark lines etched
below his eyes and his mouth was set in a taut
controlled line. He looked as if he hadn't slept as
well as she had.

'Which do you prefer, tea or coffee for
breakfast?' he asked.

'Tea, please,' she whispered, and sat up, shaking
her hair back behind her shoulders, feeling an urge
to reach out a hand to him, wanting to make
contact with him in some way because he seemed
so withdrawn. 'Magnus——' she began, and
actually did stretch a hand towards him.

'Get up and get dressed,' he ordered curtly. 'I'll

see you downstairs in the kitchen.' And turning on his heel he left the room.

Helen dressed quickly in Wanda's clothes again, washed in the bathroom on the second floor, examining her reflection in the mirror there, looking for changes in her appearance. Surely she should look different after what had happened? But she didn't. She looked just the same, a little pale as always, her eyes seeming very dark in contrast to her fair hair. Only her lips looked changed. They were more pink than usual.

In the kitchen Magnus was sitting at the table eating cereal and consulting what seemed to be a timetable of some sort.

'Tea is made,' he said laconically, not looking at her. 'You'll have to make do with cereal.'

Helen poured her tea, filled a dish with cereal and poured milk on it, then sat down.

'Where do you have to be by the end of today?' she asked matter-of-factly, although that wasn't what she really wanted to ask him. She wanted to say to him *What's the matter? Why are you so cold, so indifferent this morning? Who are you today?*

'Rome,' he replied.

'Oh, can you get there today?'

'If I'm lucky. If I can get to Glasgow Airport in time to catch a shuttle flight at a few minutes past twelve that will get me to Heathrow with plenty of time to spare to change terminals and book on a flight to Rome this evening,' he replied coldly, and gave her a critical glance. 'I should have left here yesterday evening to make sure of getting to Rome today, but you weren't very co-operative. You would insist on having a *decent* meal before you went anywhere. And after that everything got out of control.'

'Well, it wasn't my fault,' she retorted. '*I* didn't drink too much whisky or too much wine. *I* didn't have to go for a walk to clear my head. *I* was quite ready to leave after we'd eaten. And that was why I went upstairs to look for you to ask you if you would take me to the mainland. And if you'd told me you wanted to go to Glasgow, and why, I might have been more disposed to co-operate with you. Why didn't you?'

'Why should I?' he countered, pushing his chair back and rising to his feet. 'I thought you'd be so glad to leave when I suggested that we go that you'd jump at the chance. Now hurry up, or I'll leave without you and you'll be here all alone until Isabel Macleish comes to do the cleaning.' He stepped over to the porch and came back with Wanda's boots and yellow waterproof and dropped them on the floor beside her. 'Hurry up,' he ordered again, his voice crisping. 'And be ready to go when I come back. I'm just going to throw a few things into a bag and then I'm off.'

He strode from the room, and after glaring at his unsuspecting back as if she would have liked to have hit him Helen finished her cereal and tea. By the time he came back to the kitchen she was ready and was standing by the porch door wearing her own rather shrunken but dry shoes and the yellow waterproof and was carrying her dried clothing in a plastic bag she had found in one of the kitchen drawers.

Across the moors they walked separately, Magnus in front, his zipped holdall slung over one shoulder, Helen behind him wishing there was more time to enjoy the sunshine and the scenery. She always seemed to be crossing the island in a hurry, with no time to stand and stare at the beauties of nature. The small bay was flat, mirroring everything perfectly, the stones of the jetty, the puffy white clouds sailing across the blue sky. But there was no black motorboat tied up there.

'Where's the boat?' Helen exclaimed. 'Oh, surely it hasn't been washed away again! There wasn't much wind last night.'

'No, it hasn't been washed away,' Magnus replied coolly, dropping his holdall down on the jetty. 'It never was washed away. I always put it in the boathouse when I've finished with it for the day.'

'Oh, so that's where it was on Saturday night?'

'That's where it was,' he remarked, giving her a sardonic look. 'Wait here while I go and get it.'

'Magnus Scott, you're ... you're the most deceitful, selfish, arrogant. . . .'

She broke off, because he hadn't stayed to listen to her tirade but was striding back along the jetty towards the path which curved round the bay to the boathouse. She watched him go, her breast still heaving with indignation, thinking of the many ways in which he had deceived her that weekend. He hadn't actually told any lies. He had just avoided answering her truthfully when she had asked direct questions. The only real lie had been his impersonation of Blair, because the castle did belong to a relative both of Magnus and Blair, Magnus's mother and Blair's mother-in-law, and in a way while he stayed at the castle Magnus was the caretaker. When Helen told him the boat had been washed away he hadn't denied that it had, but he hadn't seemed very worried either, and when she had asked him where he had found it he had said it didn't matter where. All that mattered was that he had found it and was able to rescue her.

But what about the rest, about last night and all the talk about loving her more than any other woman he had loved before? It was beginning to look as if that had been a lie, a deliberate one just to get her to give in to him, to get what he wanted from her, because if he had meant it he wouldn't want her to leave now, would he? He'd keep her a prisoner here and they'd live on kisses and lemon pudding. Her lips quivered into a smile at the remembrance of his nonsense.

The roar of the motorboat's engine starting up drew her attention and she looked across the bay. It was coming towards the jetty. In a few minutes it swerved around the end of the short protective wall and stopped at the steps. She handed the holdall and the plastic bag to Magnus and then stepped aboard.

Across the strait of water, limpid blue this morning and deceptively still, not seeming at all dangerous, the boat swooped noisily, shattering the Sunday morning quiet. Turning in her seat, Helen looked back at Carroch, watching the island grow smaller and a little misty. Never would she see it again, yet she would always remember the two nights and a day she had spent there with the dangerously attractive, mercurial Magnus. Never would she forget him.

The boat turned into the protection of the jetty on the mainland and stopped beside a sturdy varnished fishing boat which was tied up there. A fresh-faced man of about thirty years of age, dressed in a tartan shirt, jeans and seaboots, came down the jetty and caught the rope Magnus threw to him. When he had tied the rope to one of the iron rings in the jetty the young man came back and gave Helen a hand to help her out of the boat and up the steps.

'Good morning, miss,' he said cheerfully. 'I'm Archie Macleish. How are ye this morning, Magnus?' he called out as he caught the holdall Magnus had thrown up to him. 'And what kept you last night? I was waiting for ye to come across until nearly midnight.'

'Sorry, Archie,' replied Magnus as he came up the steps. 'There was something I had to do before leaving the castle, so we came across as soon as we could this morning. Did you manage to get the car open.'

'I did that,' said Archie. They all began to walk along the jetty towards the cottage. 'I used a wire coathanger.' He turned to Helen with a rueful grin. 'I hope ye won't be minding, miss. I had to pull away a little of the rubber protection around one of the windows to get the wire through, then I was able to hook the wire round the lever of the lock and pull it up. But you can always get that fixed, and I was thinking ye'd rather be able to get into the car than not. Now starting the engine without the key was a different matter,' he continued, turning back to Magnus. 'It's a case of crossing wires together. But come on, let me show you.'

When they reached the car Archie opened the trunk and showed them which two wires to cross to start the engine, warning them to keep the engine going once he had started it or they might not get it started again. Then Helen got into the driver's seat, Magnus put his holdall in the back seat and slid into the passenger seat beside her.

'You won't mind giving me a lift to the airport,

will you? I believe it's on your way home,' he said coolly.

'No, I don't mind,' she replied, equally coolly. They said goodbye to Archie and drove off along the narrow road that twisted away from the sea past lush green meadows, where Highland cattle grazed before climbing up to brown, rock-scattered moorland where flocks of sheep nibbled at heather. By the time they reached the junction with the main road to Lochgilphead Magnus was fidgeting with impatience, and Helen wasn't surprised when he asked her to stop.

'Why?' she demanded, continuing to drive.

'Because I want to get to the airport before noon. The plane leaves soon afterwards, and the rate you're going we'll be lucky if we get there tomorrow,' he jibed sarcastically.

'I can't drive any faster along this road,' she retorted. 'There are too many bends.'

'But I can drive faster,' he replied. 'Come on, stop and let's change places. Let me drive, Eilidh, please.'

'Oh, all right,' she muttered ungraciously, and stopped the car on the shoulder of the road. 'Do you have a licence?'

'Of course I have a licence. I just don't have a car.'

'Then how did you get to the jetty at Archie Macleish's cottage so that you could cross to Carroch?' she asked.

'By a very slow and tortuous route, by train to Oban where Archie picked me up in his van. Now move over into this seat so I can get into that one. And hurry up, we've wasted enough time already.'

He got out of the door on the passenger side and went round to the door on her side and opened it. She didn't move.

'Eilidh,' he said menacingly, 'are you going to move or am I going to shove you over?'

'I think you're the most domineering, selfish. . . .'

'Deceitful egotist you've ever met,' he finished for her with a wicked glint. 'You see how well you've got to know me after all? And yet last night you said you didn't know me. Now come on Eilidh, love—move, or I'll miss that plane.'

Helen moved, and he got into the seat beside her and revved the engine quickly because it was in danger of stopping. The car swerved out on to the road and was soon zooming along. He did drive fast, thought Helen as she hastily fastened the seatbelt. He drove like the madman he was, she thought viciously, flinging the little car at the bends and often taking the bends on the wrong side of the road, taking a chance on there being nothing coming from the opposite direction.

'Oh, I think you're mad, quite mad!' she gasped. 'And I wish I'd never met you!'

'I wish I'd never met you too,' he retorted.

'You've only yourself to blame for that,' she replied.

'I know, I know. I'm always to blame for anything that happens to me,' he said dryly. 'One of these days maybe I'll learn to draw back instead of rushing forward impulsively to help someone who asks for help. I'll stand back and let them go their own way. Next time Wanda . . . or any other friend of mine who wants help . . . I'll say *No, what sort of a fool do you take me for*?'

Bitterness grated in his voice and she slanted a troubled glance in his direction.

'I'm sorry,' she sighed. 'I shouldn't have said what I did. I didn't really mean it.'

He took time to glance sideways at her, a faint smile curling his lips. Reaching out his left hand, he took hold of her right hand and squeezed it gently, then raised it to his lips to kiss it briefly.

'I didn't mean it either,' he said softly. 'I'm glad I've met you, Eilidh. I was going through a very dark period of my life and you came to light it up.'

'I suppose you're going to Rome to start making the film with Leo Rossi and Marta Nielsen,' she said.

'That's right.'

'How long will it take to make?'

'It depends how well we all perform. Six months, nine months, possibly a year.' He shrugged. 'Tell me, when you get back to Glencross will you tell Blair where you've been? Will you tell him you've been with me on Carroch?'

She thought about that, looking out through the windscreen at the rolling green hills and tawny moorland rising to distant purple-headed mountains, at the glint of blue water as they approached the shores of the great sea loch Loch Fyne and turned to follow its course as it delved inland, into the heart of the mountains of Argyll.

'No, I won't tell him I've been with you,' she replied at last.

'So how will you explain?' he asked, slanting her a curious glance.

'I'll just tell him I changed my mind about going away with him.' She paused, then added frankly, 'I was in two minds about going away with him. We hadn't arranged anything definite and I was expecting him to phone me and ask me again, when you phoned me and pretended to be him.' She paused again, then added in a whisper,

'Maybe if . . . if he'd phoned me before you did I . . . I might have refused to go away with him. Who knows?'

Magnus didn't say anything, but she knew he glanced at her again. They drove on in silence, the long blue loch on one side, the woods and hills on the other side. In the bright sunlight the white houses of Inverary were dazzling. Helen would have liked to have stopped and taken a walk through the old town, but she knew better than to ask Magnus. He had made up his mind what he wanted to do and come hell or high water he would do it, riding roughshod over anyone who came in his way, using anyone who happened to be around to get where he wanted to be, just as he was using her and her car to get to Glasgow Airport. He was like that—and now she knew something else about him.

Through the mountain passes at the head of Loch Fyne they drove, always maintaining a fairly good speed because there was little traffic on the roads at that time on a Sunday. Later there would be cars, people out from the big city, driving out to look at the majestic scenery of Glen Croe. At Arrochar, instead of turning right to follow the road along which she had driven on Saturday and which follows the curve of Loch Long, Magnus drove right across the narrow isthmus of land which divides Long Loch from Loch Lomond to take the slightly shorter route to Dumbarton.

'Oh, ye'll tak' the high road and I'll tak' the low road,
And I'll be in Scotland afore ye,
But me and my true love will never meet again
On the bonnie, bonnie banks o' Loch Lomon'.'

The words of the old Scottish ballad sang through Helen's mind as she stared out at the sun-shimmered water of the long lake, seeming to mock her. She and Magnus would never meet again, here on the Banks of Loch Lomond or anywhere else, she was quite sure of that. Once he had left her to fly south, once he became involved in his own work, in the business of acting in a film, he would soon forget her and she would be only one of the many women he had condescended to love for a short time.

But she didn't want him to forget her. She wanted him to remember as she would their strange brief and wild affair. She turned towards him urgently.

'Magnus,' she whispered, and could say no more, because something rose within her, choking off her voice.

'Mmm?' He didn't look at her because they were approaching Dumbarton now and there was more traffic.

'Nothing,' she muttered. 'It doesn't matter.' Pride suddenly asserted itself, coming between her and him and insisting that she should not betray how she felt about him at that particular point in time. She wasn't the type to cling. The time of parting was close, and soon he would go his way and she would go hers and it would all be over. Life would go on.

So in silence they finished their journey, crossing the River Clyde by the bridge at Erskine, and driving across the flat land of Renfrewshire to the airport. Sunlight glittered on glass and concrete of buildings, on the fuselages of aircraft and on the many cars in the car-park. Magnus stopped the car at the kerb in front of the main entrance.

'As soon as I get out you'd better get into this seat and put your foot on the accelerator so that the engine doesn't stop,' he ordered in his most autocratic manner, and she obeyed while he opened the back door and took his holdall from the back seat.

'Thanks for the lift,' he said casually, bending to look in at her.

'Magnus ... Magnus ... is that all?' she whispered, when what she really wanted to do was to screech at him, '*Don't forget me, oh, please don't forget me. Please remember me!*'

'That's all, Eilidh,' he replied softly, and bending closer towards her kissed her hard on the lips. 'Have a safe trip home.'

He slammed the door closed and turning away walked into the building. She watched him go through a blur of tears.

'You can't park here, miss. You'll have to move on.' An airport official was looking in at her, through the slightly open window. 'You all right, miss?' he added, looking suddenly concerned. He was about as old as her father and had a kind face with grey eyes twinkling under bushy eyebrows.

'Yes, thanks. I'm fine, just fine, and I'm moving on,' she replied with a smile which cost her a great effort.

She hardly noticed the drive to Glencross as she performed each action automatically, shifting the gear lever, using the brake, turning on to the right roads by instinct. She drove straight to the block of flats where she lived, parked the car and then found the caretaker and explained that she had lost her keys. He went up to the flat with her and opened the door for her, promising he would have a new key for her the next day. Helen went in and closed the door behind her, standing still for a moment and looking round, glad to be there in the place where she could be herself, where she didn't have to pretend. Everything was just as she had left it; just as if she hadn't been away.

Again pride stepped in and dictated that she shouldn't give way to the emotions which were churning through her, threatening to demoralise her. There was much to do—clothes to change, a meal to be made, telephoning to do. Not until she had bathed, put on some of her own clothes and had eaten a sandwich and drunk some coffee did she make the first of her telephone calls. She dialled Blair's number and a stranger answered, a woman who spoke softly without any Scottish accent.

'Dr Calder's residence.'

'May I speak to Dr Calder, please?' asked Helen.

'Who is that calling, please?' answered the woman coolly.

'I . . . is Mrs Gibson, his housekeeper, there?' Helen parried.

'No. This is Mrs Calder speaking. Dr Calder is out at the moment. May I take a message for him?'

Mrs Calder. Wanda was at Blair's house, then? Helen hesitated not sure whether she should tell Blair's wife who she was. Eventually she said rather weakly,

'Oh, no. It's all right,' and put the receiver down.

She was staring at the telephone, wondering what to do next, wondering why Wanda was still at Blair's house, when the doorbell of the flat rang. She hurried over to the door and opened it. Blair

Calder stood in the corridor. He was dressed in a neat grey three-piece suit, his reddish hair was smoothly brushed as always, but his hazel eyes held an anxious expression.

Helen—thank heaven!' he exclaimed, stepping past her into the room. 'Where have you been?' he demanded.

'Away,' she said vaguely as she shut the door.

'Away where?' he asked angrily, frowning at her.

'To ... to ... stay with a friend,' she replied, going past him into the living room. 'Won't you sit down? Would you like a drink? I've not long since made coffee.'

'I think I need something stronger than coffee,' he muttered, rubbing his forehead.

'I'm afraid I don't have any spirits,' she said. 'But do sit down, Blair. You look awfully upset about something.'

'Upset! Upset?' he exclaimed, pacing away from her and then swinging round to face her. 'Upset is putting it mildly! Here I've been nearly out of my mind wondering what had happened to you, wondering why you weren't here when I called in on Friday afternoon to pick you up so we could go away together, and all you can do is tell me I look upset! Of course I'm upset! You ... well, you practically stood me up, by going away without letting me know where you'd gone or why.'

'Yes, I suppose it must look like that to you,' said Helen quietly as she sank down into a chair. 'But you see ... when you didn't phone me again after Monday I thought that perhaps you'd changed your mind. Or that perhaps you weren't able to get away for the weekend.' She looked directly at him. 'You did say on Monday that you would phone me and tell me what time you'd be picking me up and where we would be going, you know. Why didn't you?'

'I ... I ... something happened,' he said, turning away from her, pacing to the door of the flat and then coming back to look at her. 'You could have waited,' he went on. 'I was here about two and I remember distinctly telling you when we talked about going away on Monday that we should try to get away by one o'clock on Friday. Surely you could have waited a while ... or got in touch to find out why I was late? You could have phoned me.' He frowned at her. 'Instead you went off without having the politeness to leave a message. I thought perhaps you'd gone down to see your parents, so I phoned them.'

'You shouldn't have done that, Blair,' Helen objected quietly. 'They ... I haven't told them I've been going out with you. Who did you talk to? My father or my mother?'

'Your mother.'

'Did you tell her you'd planned to take me away for the weekend?'

'No, I did not,' he snapped. 'I'm not that much of a fool. I just said that I'd had a date with you and had called for you but you weren't in your flat and no one seemed to know where, so I thought you must have gone to see your parents.'

'What did she say?'

'She said she wasn't expecting you this weekend, but if you did turn up she would tell you I'd phoned. Then she rang off.' Blair managed to look very offended. 'She was very cool and offhand and didn't seem at all upset.'

'I'm glad. I wouldn't have wanted her or my father to have been worried about me,' said Helen, feeling a sense of relief because he had failed to disturb her mother, thankful that Janet Melrose was always unflappable. 'Still, I wish you hadn't got in a tizzy and phoned them.'

'You're taking all this very coolly, Helen,' he said raspingly, sitting down on the sofa. 'You don't seem to realise you owe me an explanation for your behaviour.'

'But I've already explained. I thought you must have changed your mind about going away for the weekend and when I didn't hear from you I went by myself,' she retorted, feeling her own temper rising in reaction to his overbearing attitude.

'Without leaving a message for me.'

'How could I leave a message for you? Where and with whom was I supposed to leave it?' she countered. 'No one is supposed to know we've been meeting regularly. We've tried to keep our association a secret. At least, I have. I . . . I'm not sure about you.'

Blair's eyes flickered and his narrow pale face flushed slightly and he looked away from her. In that moment Helen knew that Magnus had been telling the truth when he had said Blair hadn't kept his association with her a secret from Wanda, and the last of her liking for Blair died a quick and painless death.

'Where did you go?' he demanded jealously, changing the direction of the conversation.

'I've told you—I went to see a friend. Oh, I wish you'd stop going on about it!' she snapped, letting her anger with him break through. 'I'm free to go where I like when I like. I don't have to tell you everything. I'm not your wife!'

Again he looked uncomfortable, his face flushing a dull red, and she wondered why she had ever thought he was handsome. Compared with Magnus he seemed dull and old, even though he could be only four or five years older than his half-brother-in-law.

'Helen, there's something I have to tell you,' he announced abruptly, pacing away from her. 'Wanda came, on Friday afternoon, just when I was going to leave to come here to pick you up. She's still there. She . . . well, she won't go away.'

'Oh, but I thought. . . .' Helen broke off sharply, biting her lower lip. She had been about to say she thought he and Wanda had had a row and that Wanda had left the house in a huff, but realised just in time that if she did she would betray the fact that she knew more than she was supposed to know. She would betray the fact that she had been with someone who knew what had happened between Blair and his wife on Saturday morning. 'I suppose she came to discuss the divorce with you,' she muttered.

'She came to tell me she doesn't want a divorce,' Blair replied, turning and pacing back to her. 'She wants to end our separation.' He gave her a worried glance. 'I'm afraid she knows I've been seeing you, Helen, and I told her outright that I didn't want her back, that I want a divorce so I can marry you.'

'Oh dear, you shouldn't have done that. I wish you hadn't done that,' said Helen with a sigh.

'But don't you see it was the only way I could convince her that I . . . I have a good reason for wanting to divorce her?' he argued.

'Was she convinced?'

'I thought she was at first, because she went off in a huff. But she came back again later and now she won't leave.' He sat down again beside her and tried to take hold of her hands. 'Helen, I don't know what to do to make her leave, but I still want you very badly. We'll have to wait a wee while, be patient. I'm sure that now she knows about you Wanda will come round and will agree to let me divorce her.'

'No, no!' Helen sprang to her feet and walked away from him. 'I . . . I've changed my mind. I'm not in love with you and never have been, and I don't want to marry you even if you do get a divorce. Now will you please go away? Go home, go back to Wanda, and tell her that you and I aren't going to be married even if she does let you have a divorce. Go back and tell her you're glad she's come back to you and that she wants to end your separation.'

'What's the matter with you?' exclaimed Blair, getting to his feet and walking over to her. He studied her face and then shook his head from side to side. 'Usually you're so calm, so equable . . . that's why I've always liked being with you. You're so different from Wanda. But you've changed. You're different.' He frowned at her. 'Helen, where have you been? Who have you been with this weekend?' His eyes grew sharp and his lips thinned. 'Have you been with another man? Answer me, damn you! Have you been with . . . with a lover?'

'I've told you, I've been with a friend,' she retorted. 'Now will you please go, Blair, or . . . or I'll phone your wife and tell her you've been bothering me.'

'Good God!' He stepped away from her hastily. 'You wouldn't do that?'

'I will if you won't go away and leave me alone.'

'You're upset because Wanda has turned up, I

can see that,' he wheedled. 'But she won't stay. She never has. She'll get bored and will want to go back to London. We'll talk again tomorrow when you're feeling better. I'll see you at the hospital.'

'No, Blair, no! I don't want to see you again. I don't want to meet you anywhere. Now will you please go away and leave me alone, or I'll phone Wanda and tell her you're here!'

'All right, all right, I'll go,' he said testily, stalking towards the door. 'Come to think of it, I don't really want to see you again, since you stood me up on Friday to go away with someone else,' he jibed nastily. 'You're not at all the person I thought you were. Not at all!'

He opened the door, stepped out into the corridor and closed the door behind him. Alone again, Helen let out a sigh of relief. Now it was up to Wanda.

CHAPTER SIX

HELEN didn't sleep well that night. Her emotions were too churned up, and she spent hours examining and trying to analyse her own behaviour when she had been with Magnus, wondering if she really had fallen in love with him or if what had happened had been merely a brief flare-up of sexual passion and nothing more. Then when she wasn't doing that she was worrying about Blair's behaviour, his insistence that he still wanted to marry her if he could persuade Wanda to agree to a divorce.

She fell asleep eventually as dawnlight slanted through the window and was wakened from the heavy slumber when her alarm clock went off at seven instead of the usual seven-thirty. Heavy-eyed, she stared at the clock, wondering why she had set it to ring half an hour earlier, then she remembered that she would have to catch the bus to work instead of going by car because she wasn't sure if she could start the car in the way that Archie Macleish had shown her.

Her weekend away had certainly given her plenty to think about and plenty of problems to solve, she thought wryly, but she had no time while she was at work to think about anything but testing and analysing samples of blood, urine and various tissues taken from various human bodies. And she was glad there was a lot for her to do, since the other lab technician was away for a week on holiday, because it meant she stayed in the laboratory and there was no chance of her running into Blair if he should happen to be in the hospital.

She left the hospital as usual at four-thirty and caught a bus back to the seaside town where she lived, then she called in at the petrol garage on the corner of the street to ask what she should do about getting another key to start her car. The proprietor of the garage was helpful and said he would try to obtain one from the dealer in that particular make of car in Glasgow. Helen left details of the year and model of the car with him and then walked to her flat.

The phone was ringing when she entered and she rushed across to it to answer, then hesitated, hoping it wasn't Blair who was ringing. Slowly she picked up the receiver and spoke cautiously.

'Hello,' she said.

'Helen, how are you?' Janet Melrose's voice was warm and affectionate, and Helen sank down on to an armchair with a sigh of relief.

'I'm fine, Mother, thank you. I hope everything is all right with you and Dad. It isn't like you to phone at this time of the day.'

'I was a wee bit worried about you,' said Janet, 'so I thought I'd ring just to make sure you were back from wherever you went for the weekend.'

'I got back yesterday about one o'clock,' replied Helen.

'Well, I must tell you that a Dr Calder phoned here, late on Friday night and then again on Saturday. He wanted to know if you were here. He seemed to be very upset because you weren't at your flat when he called to see you there. I told him I would pass the message on to you if you came home but that I wasn't expecting you. On Saturday he was so worried that he said he was thinking of asking the police to look out for your car and asked our permission to do so. Have you seen him since you came back?'

'Yes, I have, and everything is straightened out now. It wasn't important. How is everything with you?'

'I'm looking forward to the summer holidays. We finish school at the end of the month, and your father and I are going to the cottage at Kilford as soon as we can. Will you be coming down as usual in July for your holiday?'

'Yes, I will.'

'Good. I'll ring off now—time to be getting the tea ready. Goodbye.'

''Bye, Mum, and thanks for ringing.'

Soothed by her mother's placid manner, Helen replaced the receiver and went through to the small bedroom to change from her skirt and blouse into something more casual. As she pulled on jeans and T-shirt she noticed another pair of jeans and a blouse on the chair in her room. Wanda Murray's clothes. What should she do with them? Return them to their owner, of course, if Wanda was still at Blair's house.

It would be a good way of making contact with Wanda, she thought as she went into the kitchenette to make some tea for herself, and perhaps she should talk to the woman and tell her that no matter what Blair said she wasn't going to marry him. And it would be good to talk to someone who knew Magnus and who would perhaps tell her more about him. Plugging in the kettle, she left the kitchenette and went straight to the phone and dialled the unlisted number of

Blair's private residence. The housekeeper answered the phone.

'I was wondering,' said Helen, 'if Mrs Calder is still staying there.'

'Yes, she is.'

'I'd like to speak to her, please.'

There was a clatter at the other end of the line as the receiver was put down. A few seconds later it was picked up and the soft musical voice of Wanda spoke.

'Mrs Calder, I'm Helen Melrose. I . . . I believe you've heard of me.'

'I certainly have.' The voice hardened, took on an icy tone. 'And I think you've a real nerve to phone me! I have nothing to say to you. . . .'

'Mrs Calder—oh, please wait a moment,' said Helen hurriedly, guessing that Wanda was about to hang up on her. 'I . . . have something of yours that I'd like to return to you.'

'Something of mine?' exclaimed Wanda. 'I don't understand how you have something of mine. Look, is this some sort of trick?'

'No, honestly. I have some clothes of yours and. . . .'

'Clothes? How did you get some of my clothes? Don't tell me you've stayed here in this house and taken some of them! Well, if you have, I'm going to sling some mud at your name! I'm going to make sure everyone knows what a sneaking little thief you are—trying to steal my husband from me, taking my clothes. . . .'

'Oh, please, please stop!' Helen found she was having to shout to make herself heard. 'I've never stayed at Blair's house and I haven't stolen anything. Please listen to me. I was at Carroch Castle at the weekend with Magnus Scott, your half-brother, and . . . well, I fell in the sea and lost my suitcase and all my clothes and he lent me some of yours, so. . . .'

'You've been with Magnus on Carroch?' Wanda's voice rose in surprise, then she added quickly. 'Where are you now?'

'At my flat. It's in Seakirk, just along the coast from Glencross.'

'I know, I know,' said Wanda impatiently. 'There's a big hotel there. The Marina, it's called.'

'That's right.'

'Can you get to the hotel—easily, I mean?'

'Yes, I can.'

'I'll meet you in the lounge of the hotel at about seven o'clock,' said Wanda quickly. 'Bring my clothes with you—I think I'd like to meet you after all. I must go now. See you later.'

She hung up and the line went dead. Bewildered, feeling as if a strong wind had swept through the room and whirled her around, Helen hung up too and went back to the kitchenette. Wanda, it seemed, was even more mercurial than Magnus!

At quarter to seven, having changed again, into a summer dress over which she wore a cardigan, she walked down the street towards the esplanade. The evening was pleasant and quite warm after a day of sunshine and the waters of the Firth of Clyde were a soft blue, ruffled here and there to darker patches by the evening breeze and scattered with the white shining triangles of sails as small boats from the sailing club took part in the Monday night race. Beyond the shimmering water the hills of Cowal behind Dunoon were green and tawny against the blue sky, and between those hills and the island of Bute the Kyle of Bute, a strait of water, glimmered invitingly, seeming to point the way like a blue-grey arrow towards other hills, misty purple in the distance.

The hotel called the Marina was a stately stone building set back from the wide pavement of the esplanade and overlooking the slopes of green grass between it and the waters of the Firth. Helen had been in it only once, when she had gone to the hospital staff's Christmas party the year before which had been held in the big ballroom renowned for the excellence of its dance floor. Now she entered the foyer through the revolving door and asked a footman, who was standing just inside, where the lounge was. He directed her through a wide archway on the left into a room with wide windows overlooking the Firth. It was furnished with round tables and chairs and there was a bar at one end. Only one person was in the room and she was easily recognisable as Wanda Murray or Calder, her halo of red-gold hair glowing about her pretty heart-shaped face. She was dressed discreetly in a beautifully tailored suit of navy blue linen with touches of white at the neck and wrists and she was talking pleasantly to the barman, as she perched on one of the stools at the bar.

Helen went over to the bar and Wanda broke off what she was saying to turn and look at her. Her blue eyes, which were not quite the same dense blue as Magnus's, widened in amazement.

'You're not ... you can't be ... Helen?' she whispered, then gave the barman a wary glance. Taking the hint, he turned his back to them and began to rearrange some bottles on the shelves at the back of the bar, whistling to himself.

'Yes, I am,' said Helen. Now that she was face to face with Wanda she felt very nervous, totally out of her depth in the presence of such cool sophistication. 'I . . . I've brought your clothes,' she said, and offered the brown paper parcel to Wanda.

'Oh, yes. Thank you, thank you,' said Wanda hastily, ignoring the parcel as she slid off the high stool. 'Let's go and sit over there by the window, it should be private enough. But perhaps you'd like a drink first?' She was holding a cocktail glass half full of some pale liquor in one hand.

'No, thanks,' said Helen.

They went over to the table by the window and sat down. Across the table Wanda studied Helen frankly.

'Oh God,' she muttered suddenly, holding a slender white hand to her forehead as if she had a pain there. Several rings glittered on her long fingers. 'This is far worse than I'd expected. I'd no idea you'd be like you are. I thought you'd be . . . er. . . .'

'A hard-faced sex kitten,' Helen supplied with a little smile.

'Well, yes.'

'That's what Magnus said too.'

'I'd no idea you'd be so young and fresh-looking, so innocent.' Wanda gulped at her drink. 'How old are you exactly?'

'Twenty-two—almost twenty-three. Actually I look younger than I am,' said Helen.

'Yes, you do. It's your perfect complexion and the way you wear your hair, I suppose,' murmured Wanda, and shook her head from side to side, 'Oh, my dear, why?' she went on. 'Why go for a married man who has a daughter who's half your age? Couldn't you find someone younger, someone who's single? I've no intention of giving Blair up, you know, just so that you can marry him.'

'I ... I don't want you to give him up,' whispered Helen. 'I don't want to marry him. I ... well, the truth is it was all his idea—marriage, I mean. He said ... or he's kept on saying ... that as soon as he could get a divorce from you he would be free to marry me.'

'I see.' Wanda leaned back in her chair, her rather full lips curving into a cynical smile. 'He says that to all the girls,' she said dryly. 'It's his great line, his way of intriguing them, you could call it, holding their interest in him.'

'I ... Mrs Calder, I want you to know I wouldn't have gone out with him, continued to see him all these past months if ... if he hadn't said his marriage to you was a farce and that he hoped to end it. Honestly, I wouldn't.'

'You were sorry for him?' asked Wanda.

'Yes, I suppose I was.'

'You're not the first, but I'm going to make damn sure you're the last,' said Wanda, her voice hardening. 'That's why I'm here and why I'm staying. I love Blair and I know he loves me, and I've told him I won't let him divorce me. So leave him alone, Helen Melrose, stay away from him!'

'Oh, I will, I will. I have every intention of doing that,' said Helen quickly. 'But the question is, will he leave me alone, will he stay away from me? Did you know he came to see me yesterday?'

'When?' demanded Wanda, looking very puzzled.

'Soon after I'd returned from ... from Carroch. He told me you had come and were staying at his house and he said he was sure you would go away soon and that he would be able to wear you down, get you to agree to a divorce, and that we had only to be patient. ...'

'Did you believe him?' demanded Wanda.

'I . . . no, not any more. And I told him that I don't want to marry him even if he does get a divorce. I told him to go away and leave me alone, but he wouldn't believe me. The only way I could get rid of him was to threaten to phone you and tell you he was harassing me.'

Wanda stared for a moment, blankly, as she absorbed what Helen had said, then her blue eyes began to twinkle and she put back her head and laughed.

'Oh, this is priceless!' she spluttered after a while as she dabbed at her eyes with a handkerchief. 'It's so funny, when you stop to think about it.' She sobered and looked across at Helen. 'But I hope you've learned something and haven't been too hurt in the process, Helen. Blair is . . . well, I suppose you could call him an habitual philanderer. He can't help flirting with any pretty woman that he comes into contact with: nurses, women doctors, sometimes patients. He does it, I realise, because he's not sure of me; because he can't be sure I'm not flirting with the men I meet in the course of following my career. He does it to get my attention, and it never fails.'

'That's what Magnus said,' agreed Helen.

'Ah, yes, Magnus.' Wanda's eyes narrowed as she studied Helen's face first, then looked at the brown paper parcel. She pulled the parcel towards her and slipped the string off it and opened it. 'Yes, these are mine,' she said thoughtfully, lifting each garment in turn. 'I usually leave a few clothes in my closet at Carroch Castle so that I don't have to carry much with me when I'm going there.' She looked across at Helen again. 'Are you going to tell me what you were doing at Carroch?'

'Magnus enticed me to go there.'

'Enticed you?' exclaimed Wanda. 'Good grief! Why did he do that?'

'He said that you'd asked him to help you by preventing me from going away with Blair for the weekend so that you'd be sure of finding Blair at home when you went to see him.'

'Mmm, I think I did say something like that. You see, I knew ... at least, I'd found out that both you and Blair had the weekend free and Blair's housekeeper had told me he planned to go to the Trossachs, and I suspected you might be going with him. And Magnus did say he'd do something about it.' Wanda's eyes began to dance with amusement again. 'What did he do? Please tell me.'

'Magnus asked me not to tell anyone,' Helen began hesitantly.

'You can tell me,' said Wanda persuasively. 'You have to now that I know you've been on Carroch with him.'

Helen explained quickly, starting with the telephone call she had received on Friday morning and ending with leaving Magnus at Glasgow Airport. She spoke quickly and concisely without any reference to her personal relationship with Magnus.

'Oh, how like Magnus to do something like that!' said Wanda with a sigh. 'He could have got himself into serious trouble, impersonating Blair and then making you stay with him on Carroch. I hope you're not going to lay any charges of abduction against him, Helen.' Wanda looked suddenly very anxious.

'No, I'm not. They wouldn't stick if I did. I went to Carroch willingly, thinking Blair had invited me and it was the bad weather on Friday night that made it impossible to get away then.'

'But you could have left Saturday even after you'd been swamped in the dinghy. You could have left with Max and the others, wearing my clothes since you'd lost your own. Why didn't you?' asked Wanda.

'I . . . it just didn't turn out that way. I. . . I was asleep when they left,' mumbled Helen, unable to sustain the shrewd regard of Wanda's blue eyes. 'I . . . I had to wait until Magnus wanted to leave to bring me to the mainland in the motorboat,' she added rather lamely.

'Do you know where he was going when you left him at the airport?' asked Wanda.

'He said he was going to Rome.'

'Well, that's something good that's come out of this latest escapade of his,' said Wanda. 'We . . . that is, my mother and I . . . were beginning to think he'd become a recluse, and that he would never leave Carroch and go back to acting in films again. He's been there for over three months, you know.'

'No, I didn't know. He didn't say how long he'd been there,' replied Helen. 'Why did you think he would never go back to acting in films?'

'Because he kept saying he was fed up with the whole business,' said Wanda. 'He had a pretty bad experience when he was in Hollywood. It concerned a woman, of course.' Her mouth twisted wryly. 'But I was really shocked to find out what a state he was in when I went over to Carroch a few weeks ago to see him. He'd been brooding and drinking and was in the foulest of moods. That's why I told him about Blair and you and asked for his advice and help. I thought it would take his mind off his own trouble.'

'What sort of trouble was it? What happened to him in Hollywood?'

'I can see you don't keep up with the gossip in the movie magazines,' remarked Wanda dryly.

'No, I don't. I rarely see one.'

'But you know, I suppose, that Magnus was making quite a name for himself in films.'

'Yes, I've seen one of the films he's been in.'

'Well, perhaps you don't know that with that sort of success you have to put up with a lot of exposure of your private life, not so much in this country where the public tends to respect privacy but certainly in the States and especially in Hollywood, and ever since he went there, under contract to make several films for Fiedler Films, Magnus has suffered from too much publicity. Everything he's done, every date he's made with a woman has received publicity. It's all been part of the build-up of his image as a romantic leading actor. All Fiedler's doing, of course. Max Fiedler knows how to market the goods he has for sale better than anyone.' The twist to Wanda's lips was even more cynical. 'Anyway, to cut it short, last December an actress was found dead from an overdose of some drug in her Hollywood apartment. Magnus had been very friendly with her.' Wanda paused to finish her drink, then added, 'She left a note, unfortunately. It implied that Magnus had dumped her and she hadn't been able to take it.'

'Had he?' whispered Helen.

'At the inquiry into the cause of her death he said that he'd been only friends with her and nothing else, but the coroner didn't believe him—accused him of seducing the woman before leaving her and said he was to blame for her suicide.

Magnus lost his temper and told the coroner what he thought of him, implying that the coroner was using the inquiry to get publicity for himself by criticising the behaviour of a well-known film actor. The coroner blew his top and charged Magnus with slander. There was a trial, Magnus was found guilty of slander, was fined heavily and refused to pay the fine and was put in jail.'

'Oh, no!' gasped Helen. 'Oh, how foolish of him!

'You can say that again, but Magnus is like that, impulsively quixotic, and yet I have to admire him for standing up for what he believes to be right and for attacking what he believes to be wrong.'

'How long was he in jail?'

'Not long. Max Fiedler paid the fine and got him out and sent him home to cool his heels. Magnus went to Carroch.' Wanda sighed. 'It's taken him a long time to get over it. He really let the whole business get to him, almost as if he had begun to believe he was responsible for the woman's death or as if he could have prevented it if he hadn't been away from Hollywood at the time.'

'Do you think he was responsible?'

'Good grief, no! Not at all. Magnus would never treat a woman so badly that she would take her own life—at least not deliberately, not knowingly. But he's always had problems with women. The image of the romantic hero of the movie screen has attracted them to him like bees to honey, yet I don't think he's ever met one who has loved him for himself, who's fallen for the real Magnus.'

'Is there a real Magnus?' asked Helen.

'Of course there is, and I suspect you met him

on Carroch,' replied Wanda, giving Helen a direct, shrewd stare. 'How did you get on with him?'

'I'm not sure. We argued a lot at first,' replied Helen, wishing there was some way she could control her colour. Her cheeks were burning. 'He said I deflated his oversized ego.'

'Ha!' Wanda laughed delightedly. 'Good for you! I suspect he would like you, Helen. He'd find you a refreshing change from the women who butter him up all the time and expect too much from him or who try to possess him. Did you like him?'

Helen didn't reply to that immediately. 'Like' seemed too weak a word to describe her feelings with regard to Magnus.

'Not all the time,' she said at last. 'There were moments when I disliked him intensely.'

'Mmm. Sounds interesting,' drawled Wanda, her eyes beginning to twinkle again. 'But I must go.' She picked up the parcel and rose to her feet. 'Blair will be home soon and I want to be there when he arrives.' Her smile was self-mocking, giving her a fleeting resemblance to Magnus. 'I've turned over a new leaf,' she added. 'From now on I'm going to be a good wife. I've done what I had to do. I've done my thing as a performer and now I'm ready to settle down and devote myself to Blair and Ailsa—I might even have another child. Who knows?'

'Are you going to tell Blair I was with Magnus at the weekend?' Helen asked anxiously as she walked with Wanda through the foyer of the hotel.

'I might. It would be a good way of putting an end to his infatuation with you if he knew that you'd spent a night and a day with his notorious half-brother-in-law. He'd be so miffed thinking you preferred to be with Magnus than to be with him that he wouldn't have anything to do with you again. And that's what we both want, isn't it, Helen?'

'I suppose it is,' muttered Helen as she followed Wanda through the revolving door and out on to the broad stone front steps. Beyond the expanse of green grass that sloped down to the edge of the water the small racing boats were sailing towards an orange marker buoy, tilting over as the wind which had increased filled their shining sails.

'But don't worry, I'll only tell Blair if I find it's necessary,' said Wanda. 'And if I do tell him, I'll swear him to secrecy. Now can I give you a lift to your flat?'

'No thanks, I'll walk. It's not far.'

'Then thanks for returning my clothes to me, and thanks for being. . . .' Wanda paused, then added with a winning smile, 'Just thanks for being you, Helen. Goodbye for now. I'm sure we're going to meet again sooner or later.'

Whether Wanda found it necessary to tell Blair that Helen had spent part of the weekend on the island of Carroch with Magnus Helen herself never knew, but during the next few days she noticed that Blair made no contact with her, and it was with a sense of relief that she heard at the beginning of the following week that he had gone away on an extended vacation and that there were rumours that he would be leaving Glencross and setting up a practice in the London area. Wanda, it seemed, had got her own way in the end.

June went out in a blaze of beautiful weather and at the end of the first week of July Helen was able to take her own annual holiday. Glad to get away for a while, hoping that staying with her parents and meeting old friends and acquaintances would enable her to recover her badly disturbed equilibrium, she drove down to Kilford, the small seaside resort on the Solway Firth where her parents had always spent the months of July and August in the stone cottage they had bought and renovated.

Everything in Kilford was the same as it had always been. The tide still went out from the river estuary as if someone had removed a plug from a drain, leaving exposed banks of shining brown mud for several hours and then returned just as swiftly and silently to cover the banks with smooth shining water. The cottage owned by Janet and William Melrose looked as always neat and white on its green hillock overlooking the old pier where, in the past, small freighters had tied up to load granite from the nearby quarry and fishing boats had found shelter, but which was now only used by members of the local sailing club as a park for their dinghies.

The people who came to Kilford every summer for their holidays were also the same, and at first Helen went about with her friends, crewing regularly for Bob Cairns, whom she had known for years and who had just finished his training to be an architect and was hoping to be employed by her father's firm. With Bob she went out every evening of the first week to the sailing club or the local pub to discuss the day's sailing with other sailors. She went on picnics and other outings, but by the beginning of the second week she realised her heart wasn't in what she was doing. Her heart was in the Highlands, on an island called Carroch, where she had lost it to a man called Magnus.

It was easy to pretend she was happy and

contented with her lot during the daytime, but the nights were bad, very bad, as she spent many hours thinking about Magnus and wishing over and over again that she could meet him again, and failing to find an answer to her wish. She couldn't go to Italy and find out where he was filming and walk in on him. She couldn't chase him, not only because she guessed he didn't like being chased by a woman but also because her own pride wouldn't let her. And he would never go out of his way to seek her out, she was sure. To do that would be too much like making a commitment for him, and he was wary of commitment.

Her holiday came to an end and she felt listless and depressed after spending hours without sleep, pining for she knew not what as she prepared to return to work. She was in her bedroom at the cottage packing her clothes on a Sunday afternoon before setting out on the two-and-a-half-hour drive north when her mother came in with a fruitcake she had baked for her to take with her.

'Bob is downstairs,' Janet announced. 'He wants to have a wee talk with you before you leave.'

'Oh, bother,' said Helen. 'I've nothing to say to him—nothing at all. Mum, can't you make an excuse for me, tell him I'm late leaving and haven't time to see him?'

'No, I cannot,' said Janet firmly. 'He's been a good friend to you over the years and I think you owe it to him to hear what he has to say.'

'But, Mother, you don't seem to realise. He's going to propose to me!'

'Of course I realise he is,' retorted Janet. 'Do you think I haven't got eyes in my head?' She looked at Helen closely, her own brown eyes narrowing. 'I thought you'd be glad,' she sighed.

'You've been looking very peaky and worried these past few days and I thought that was what was on your mind. I thought you were worried in case Bob didn't pop the question.'

'All I've been worried about is how to refuse without hurting his feelings too much,' said Helen coolly, fastening the locks on the new suitcase she had bought. 'I don't want to marry him.'

'Oh, Helen, why not?' exclaimed Janet, and sat down suddenly on the edge of the bed.

'Because I don't want to, that's why. Bob is a nice fellow and I'm very fond of him, but I can't see myself living with him. We're too alike and we'd bore each other to tears within six months.' Helen noticed the anxious expression on her mother's face. 'I hope you and Dad haven't been encouraging him,' she said sharply.

'Well, we certainly haven't *dis*couraged him,' retorted Janet. 'And you've gone about with him for so long that we just assumed that you liked him and would be happy with him.' She rose to her feet and went to the door. 'I'll go and tell him you'll be down in a few minutes, shall I?'

'Then you won't tell him. . . .' began Helen.

'No, I won't. There are some things in this life you have to do for yourself, Helen,' replied Janet tartly, more ruffled than Helen had ever seen her. 'And refusing a proposal of marriage is one of them!'

Surprised by her mother's unusual testiness, Helen finished packing and then carried her cases downstairs. Bob Cairns came into the narrow hallway. For once he wasn't dressed in sailing clothes but was wearing grey pants, an open-necked shirt and a light tweed jacket. His fairish brown hair was brushed neatly and his round rather boyish face was smiling.

'Let me carry those out for you, Helen,' he said politely, taking the cases from her. 'I'd like a word with you before you go.'

'All right,' she submitted with a sigh, and going in front of him opened the front door.

He put the cases in the back of her car which was parked out in front of the house in the wide road, which was really the main street of the small village and which was protected from the shoreline and the often flooding waters of the estuary by a sturdy stone wall.

'We can't talk here,' said Bob, looking around with a frown when Helen didn't make any effort to move but stood by the driver's door of the car as if ready to get into it. 'Let's walk along the pier.'

'I don't have much time, Bob,' she protested.

'Och, you haven't had much time for me all week!' he exploded suddenly, his grey eyes flashing.

'I've seen you nearly every day,' she reminded him.

'Aye, but there's always been other folks about. We've not had a minute by ourselves, not a minute. Are you coming now along the pier?'

Reluctantly she walked with him across the road and through the gateway. On either side of the pier stretched the *merse*, the local name for the marshy grassland which lay above the mudbanks and which was often flooded with water when the tide was in. Now that the tide was out the thick reeds and stiff grass waved in the strong breeze which was blowing upriver, flurries of silver light passing over the green. The end of the pier was standing in the narrow channel of the river, which shimmered grey and white, reflecting the sky and the clouds which were rolling across it.

'Do you have to go back to Glencross today?' asked Bob as they leaned on the wall at the end of the pier.

'Of course I do. I go back to work tomorrow,' Helen replied.

'I was thinking . . . Helen, would you mind if I came up to see you next week? I've another week's holiday before I start at Melrose and Martin's and I'd like to spend it near you.'

'No,' said Helen quietly, 'I . . . I don't think you should, Bob—I don't think it would be worth your while. Finish your holiday here. You'll have much more fun here.'

'What do you mean, it wouldn't be worth my while?' he demanded. 'We'd be able to see each other every evening. I'll probably see more of you than I've seen this past week.'

'No, I don't want you to come,' said Helen, staring down at the grey water that was swirling around the stone pillars of the pier. 'It wouldn't be fair . . . to you, I mean, for me to let you come up to Glencross. It wouldn't be fair to let you assume I'd agree to marry you if you decided to ask me.' She looked up and straight at him. 'And that's what you're hoping to do, isn't it? You want to ask me to marry you.'

'Well, yes, it is.' His fair face flushed slightly. 'How do you know?'

'My mother told me. But it's no use, Bob, it's no use you proposing. I don't want to marry you, so don't ask me,' she whispered.

There was an awkward silence while they both gazed at the water. The wind lifted Helen's fine hair and wafted it across her face, a silken screen behind which she could hide. Seagulls and terns soared and swooped, cackling and squealing. On the opposite shore thin clouds swept in a grey veil across the rounded summits of two distant mountains.

'There's someone else, isn't there?' Bob guessed shrewdly.

'Yes, I think so.'

'You think so?' he exclaimed. 'Surely you know? Is he from hereabouts?'

'No. But how can you tell?' She swept the hair away from her face to glance at him, worried now. 'How can you guess?'

'I've known you a long time, Helen,' he replied, 'but I've never seen you like you've been lately. It's hard to describe. It's as if you're not here half the time. You don't hear when I speak to you some times. You've been far away, with someone else.'

'I didn't think you ... I didn't think anyone would notice,' she whispered, staring at him, realising for the first time that he had also grown up. He wasn't the boy she had known and played with and gone sailing with for years. He was a man, ready to take on responsibilities of married life. 'I'm sorry, Bob,' she added. 'I didn't want to hurt your feelings, but it just can't be. You'll find someone else too, someone who'll say yes.'

She couldn't bring herself to say anything else, so turning away, she hurried back along the pier. Crossing the road, she ran up the pathway to the front door of the old granite cottage and into the hallway.

'Mother, Dad—I'm leaving now. Thanks for the holiday,' she called out. 'I'll give you a ring as soon as I get back to the flat to let you know I've arrived safely.'

'Helen, wait, wait a moment.' Janet appeared in

the doorway from the kitchen. 'Did he? Did Bob——?' she asked urgently.

'No, he didn't propose,' said Helen. 'I told him not to. Oh, don't look like that, Mother! It's all right, really it is. Bob knows plenty of other girls he can ask.'

'But you and he . . . you've known each other for so long. You seem so suited to each other,' argued Janet, looking worried. 'Helen, don't go yet,' she urged. 'Stay and have some tea and we'll talk about it. You've been so quiet and pale this past week, as if you've something on your mind. Perhaps you should tell your father and me about it. Perhaps we can help, give you some advice.'

She was tempted, because all her life she had been able to confide her troubles to her parents and they had listened and had offered solutions, but something stopped her this time.

'No, I don't think so,' she replied. 'As you've just said, there are some things in this life you just have to do for yourself, and solving this particular problem I have is something I have to do without help. But thanks, Mum, all the same.' She gave Janet a quick hug. 'I'll phone you later.'

Perhaps she should have stayed and told her parents about Magnus, she thought an hour later as she drove out of Castle Douglas along the road that winds through the Kirkcudbrightshire countryside, past long narrow Lock Ken, and climbed over the moors under the shadow of the hills known as the Rhinns of Kells, down to the Doon valley and the plain of Ayrshire. Perhaps talking to them would have helped to ease the tension in her mind. After all, confession was supposed to be good for the soul, wasn't it?

But how could she have told them how close she

and Magnus had been for that short while on Carroch? She couldn't have told them she had slept with him. Not only was that very private and personal, something she could never tell another person, a beautiful, natural happening that was her and Magnus's secret, but also it would shock her parents out of their minds if they learned that their well-behaved, sensible daughter, who had never given them a moment's cause for anxiety, had fallen passionately in love with a handsome film actor who had no interest in marriage. They would be horrified if they knew she had willingly made love with him and had slept all one night with him.

No, she couldn't have confided in them. The time for confiding in her parents was over. She was grown up, an adult person who could deal with her own problems, and she would have to suffer in silence, hoping that one day this raw ache, this longing to see Magnus again, to argue with him and make love with him, would gradually fade and wither.

She hoped it would, oh, she hoped it would. If it didn't she would die.

CHAPTER SEVEN

'THERE's a letter for you in today's post, Helen. It's marked Personal,' announced Jean MacIntyre as Helen walked into the laboratory office on the Thursday morning after she had returned to work. Jean's pale blue eyes, round and curious behind their glasses, surveyed Helen closely, noting the paleness of her face and the dark smudges beneath her eyes. 'You're a wee bit late this morning. What happened?'

'I ... I overslept.' Helen slipped off the linen blazer she was wearing over a summer dress of flower-printed cotton and hung it on a hanger in the clothes closet, then went over to Jean's desk. 'Where's the letter?'

'Here you are.' Jean handed her a long blue envelope. 'It must be from someone who doesn't know your home address,' she added.

'Yes, it must,' replied Helen, and slipped the envelope into one of the pockets of her white technician's coat which she had just put on. She wasn't going to open it and read it in front of the nosy Jean. 'Is Dr Mason in the lab?' she asked in a whisper, glancing towards the half open door of the laboratory.

'No, not yet. You're lucky—he's at a meeting in the administrative offices and he'll be there all morning. He'll never know you were late today ... unless Brenda tells him.' Brenda was the other technician.

'Thanks, Jean,' Helen said warmly, and went

into the laboratory. Brenda Taggart was busy at her bench and scarcely looked up from what she was doing to acknowledge Helen's greeting. Going to her own bench, Helen sat down on the stool, looked at the array of sample tubes laid out for her examination and, sighing, leaned her elbows for a moment on the bench and rested her forehead on her hands. If only she didn't feel so tired and listless! If only she could sleep properly at night instead of spending hours thinking about Magnus. She had hoped that when she returned to work she would be so busy that he would slip into the background of her thoughts and eventually be forgotten.

But it hadn't been like that these past three days. She had thought of him continually, regretting that their parting had been so abrupt, that she hadn't been able to tell him she would think of him and would hope to see him again. She had never felt like this about any man before. Was it because he had gone away? Was absence causing her to grow fonder of him? Or was this the beginning of love, the love she had read about and had hoped to feel one day? Was this agony love?

She pushed her hand in her pocket to take out a handkerchief to wipe away the tears which had sprung to her eyes and felt the stiff envelope. She drew it out and stared at it. Her name and the address of the hospital had been typewritten. The postmark was rather faint and she couldn't make out the name on it. Who would write to her at the hospital? Any of her friends or relatives who would write to her would send their letters to the address of her flat.

Quickly she slit the envelope open and took out the single sheet of matching blue notepaper, her glance going immediately to the address which was embossed in the right-hand corner. *Castle Carroch, by Barracuish, Argyllshire*. Her heart leaping suddenly with excitement, Helen glanced quickly at the signature. Boldly written, it was not the one she had hoped to see. It was not Magnus Scott but Megan Scott-Murray, Magnus's mother.

'Dear Helen Melrose,' the letter began, 'I have been hearing much about you from my daughter Wanda and also from my son Magnus and I would like very much to meet you. At present I am staying at Castle Carroch and will be there for the next two weeks. I wonder if you would care to come to the Castle next weekend (the dates were in brackets). I realise this is short notice. I would have given more, only you were not at the hospital where you work last Friday when I called there to see you and I was told you would be back at work this week.

'If you are able to come please phone the number I have enclosed and let Archie or Isabel Macleish know when you will arrive. If you do not phone I will know that you have been unable to come. Yours sincerely, Megan Scott-Murray.'

Helen stared at the signature for a long time, trying to associate it with the plump smiling white-haired woman in the photograph she had seen in Wanda's room at Castle Carroch. Then excitedly she read the letter through again. All day she thought about the invitation, wondering whether to accept it or not, wondering why Megan Scott wanted to meet her. Wanda and Magnus had both told their mother about her. Why? What had they said about her? The only way to find out would be to go, wouldn't it? And she was going, wasn't she? Of course she was. She would go, because to visit his mother would be a step closer to Magnus. She would hear something about him, what he was doing, where he was, and that would be better than spending the weekend pining for him.

She phoned the Macleish number that evening and spoke to Isabel Macleish, who said that her husband would be pleased to take Helen over to the island on Saturday afternoon. That night Helen slept better than she had for several weeks, but she couldn't get through Friday fast enough, and after packing a weekend bag and getting everything ready for an early departure on Saturday morning she couldn't sleep much Friday night for excitement and anticipation.

It was just after seven o'clock in the morning that she drove away from Seakirk and took the road north across the river Clyde to the mountains beyond. Six weeks had gone by since she had first gone that way and there were changes in the countryside. Heather bloomed, a profusion of purple spreading across the moors under the deep, more mellow glow of the August sun. Instead of blossom clusters of berries were forming on rowan trees and every garden was ablaze with dahlias and early chrysanthemums.

This time she stopped for a while in Inverary to drink coffee in the lounge of an old eighteenth-century inn before continuing along ·the road beside the waters of Loch Fyne. She still felt excited but she also felt a strange contentment. She was going back to Carroch where she had met Magnus and perhaps while she was there she would find out whether this agony of spirit and emotions she had been suffering from was really love for him.

It was just one o'clock in the afternoon when

she saw at last the Strait of Carroch, those dangerous waters which looked so blue and calm and were dotted with green islands. The Macleish cottage gleamed with reflected sunlight and the front door was open. Two children played with a sheepdog in front of the house and stared shyly at Helen when she approached the door.

Archie Macleish remembered her and welcomed her cheerfully. He took her down to the jetty and on to his varnished fishing boat. Helen would have liked to have asked him about Megan Scott-Murray and if her husband was with her at the castle, but the noise of the engine as the boat surged across the strait made conversation without shouting impossible—and then Carroch was looming before them, green and gold and earth-red, enticing them to its shores.

The stone walls of the jetty were perfectly reflected in the clear water, as was the shape of the sleek black motorboat tied up there. Archie put Helen's bag ashore, gave her a helping hand up the jetty steps, then said,

'Ye'll be able to find your own way to the castle, won't you, miss? I have to get back now. The missus wants me to drive her to Oban to visit her parents.'

'Yes, I can find the way, thank you,' Helen replied, and waited on the jetty until the fishing boat had chugged away.

In her moments of anticipation during the night she had imagined her arrival on the island. She had imagined hopefully that Magnus would have been on the jetty waiting for her. It had been wishful thinking entirely, she thought now, her lips quirking ruefully, because there was no tall figure with windblown dark hair standing on the stone wall. There was no one coming towards her along the path that twisted up through the pines either and no one coming across the moorland through the tall fronds of bracken and brown and purple branches of heather; no one in the garden where the vegetables were ready for harvesting.

Which door should she go to as an invited guest? she wondered. The front or the back? She decided on the front and walked around the old tower to the front entrance, pausing a moment to look at the view of the blue Sound stretching away to Jura and Islay, at the jumble of red rocks in the small bay, at the smooth yellow sand festooned with golden-green seaweed.

There was no bell to ring and no knocker to lift and let fall, so she tapped on the sturdy iron-studded oak door with her knuckles. No one came to open it, so she turned the iron knob and tried to push the door open. It didn't budge; presumably it was locked. After knocking again Helen gave up and wandered back to the back door and knocked on that. She was beginning to feel a little uneasy. Surely by now her hostess should be looking for her? The whole place seemed very quiet, the only sounds the lapping of the sea on the shore, the occasional cry of a bird, the rustle of leaves and grass in the light summer breeze.

No one came to answer her knock on the back door, so she turned the knob and opened it. The porch was just the same, cluttered with boots and waterproof jackets, but Magnus's jacket wasn't there, neither were his boots. Presumably they were still at the Macleishes' cottage where he had left them six weeks ago. Helen felt some of her excitement fade away. He wasn't here after all.

The kitchen was the same too, clean and tidy,

everything shining as if Isabel Macleish had just cleaned it. There were no signs of anyone having cooked a meal recently. Helen put down her overnight bag on a chair and stepped across to the hallway door.

'Hello! Is there anyone at home? I'm here, Mrs Murray,' she called out.

No reply. She stood and listened. No one moving about. Did Megan Scott-Murray go in for an afternoon nap? Or was she out walking somewhere with her husband? Helen advanced into the hallway and went into the lounge. It was also very tidy. No papers and books were scattered across the big desk. No decanter of whisky and empty glass on the coffee table. The cushions on the sofa were all plumped up and a fire had been laid in the hearth ready for lighting.

'Hello, is there anyone at home?' Back in the hallway Helen shouted from the bottom of the stairs and listened to the echo of her voice. Slowly she went up the stairs and looked in the bedroom where she had slept before—clean and tidy, untouched. The bathroom was the same and the other room, the master bedroom, where she assumed Megan Scott—Murray slept when she was at the castle, was shrouded in dust covers.

Biting her lip, feeling disappointment beginning to well up in her, Helen withdrew from the silent sunlit room and glanced up the second flight of stairs to the third-storey landing. Once again she listened intently, remembering her first evening at the castle when she had sensed she had been watched while she had looked about the place. She had that feeling now. The hairs were beginning to prickle on the back of her neck. Was there someone upstairs? Was that a floorboard creaking as someone stepped stealthily across a room?

Resisting the temptation to turn and run downstairs and leave the castle, rush out from it as she had once before, she began to go up the second flight of stairs. The landing was quiet, sunlight slanting from a high latticed window across the polished floor. From the door to Magnus's bedroom a cool draught of air wafted, drawing her attention. Hesitantly she walked towards the door and then stopped, a feeling which was a mixture of fear and excitement pulsing through her. She felt suddenly as if she was trapped in some sort of horror film. Perhaps she was dreaming she was in Castle Carroch. Perhaps she had dreamed the whole business, the arrival of the letter, the drive to the Macleishes' cottage. Perhaps it was all the result of thinking too much about Magnus and wishing she could meet him again. Perhaps she was dreaming she could hear someone whispering her name.

Someone was whispering her name! She clapped her hands to her cheeks and stared at the half-open door of Magnus's bedroom. Oh dear, she'd gone mad. She was hearing voices now!

'Eilidh, come in. Stay a while.'

There it was again, deep and strangely husky, like Magnus's voice yet not like his voice at all; hollow-sounding, like a voice she had once heard when she had gone to see the play *Hamlet* when she had been on holiday in England and had visited the theatre at Stratford-on-Avon. It was like Hamlet's father's ghost's voice. Her skin prickled again and she nearly turned and fled down the stairs.

Then the practical side of her nature asserted

itself. Impatiently she shook her head to clear it of fantasy. There were no such things as ghosts. She wasn't hearing a voice speaking to her and there was no one in Magnus's room. She would prove it. Marching forward, she pushed open the door and stepped into the room. It was neat and clean like every other room in the castle, as if Isabel Macleish had been over recently and gone through the place with a new broom, sweeping all before her. But there were no dust covers over the furniture as in the other bedrooms and a slight breeze stirred the curtains at the single lattice window. The door to the battlements was open as if someone had just stepped out on to them.

Helen didn't allow her imagination to take over again. She walked across the room and stepped through the doorway on to the wall-walk and looked first to the right and then to the left. Striped with sunlight and shadow, the wall-walk was empty. Should she walk around the tower to see if anyone was out on the battlements? Remembering what had happened to her the last time she had done that, she decided against it and closed the door firmly, deciding that Isabel Macleish had opened it, possibly to let some air into the room when she had been cleaning it and then had either forgotten to close it or hadn't closed it properly so that it had opened again.

Still keeping a control over her imagination, Helen walked back across the bedroom, averting her glance from the bed where she and Magnus had made love and had slept a few weeks ago, then leaving the room she went down the stairs, all the way down and into the kitchen. No one had come in while she had been upstairs and the room was quiet, glowing with sunlight which was shafting through the window now that the sun was in the west.

With a sigh Helen slumped down on to one of the kitchen chairs. What should she do now? Where was Megan Scott-Murray? Not staying here, certainly. The dust covers in the guest bedroom and the master bedroom were evidence of that. Opening her handbag, she took out the letter and re-read it. *At present I am staying at Carroch Castle*, Megan had written, and when Helen had phoned Isabel Macleish had been expecting to hear from her, hadn't been surprised that she had been invited to stay at the castle by its owner. And Archie had said nothing today. He hadn't said that Megan had left the castle or would be returning to it later.

Again Helen studied the signature at the bottom of the letter. It didn't look like a woman's handwriting. But then why should she jump to a conclusion like that? Many women wrote boldly, the strength of their characters showing in the way they signed their names.

Had she been hoaxed? Had someone written this letter to her and signed it with Megan's name? She jumped to her feet and went through to the lounge, straight to the desk. In the top drawer there was blue writing paper embossed with the Castle's postal address. On the top of the desk there was a selection of pens. One of them had a thick black point. Helen scribbled with it on the blue paper, then signed her own name. Written by the felt pen, it looked bold and black, unlike her usual neat flowing writing. Had Megan's signature been written by it?

She was just putting a sheet of the paper into the small portable typewriter on the desk to test if the typing of the letter she had received had been done on it when she was startled by a banging sound. She paused in what she was doing and listened. Yes, there it was again—a definite thud, thud, like someone kicking something wooden; like someone kicking at a door!

Leaving the lounge, she raced up the stairs, right up to the third storey, and paused at the top to listen again. Thud, thud. She hadn't been mistaken. Someone was kicking at the door which opened out of Magnus's room on to the battlements. Someone who had been out there when she had come up to his room before. But who? Megan Scott-Murray? Or a ghost?

The door suddenly shook violently. It wasn't being kicked this time. Someone, someone who was solid bone and muscle, had crashed into it as if hoping to burst it open.

'Oh, wait, wait!' cried Helen breathlessly, and rushing across the room she pulled the door open, just as Magnus launched himself at it again. He hurtled through the space where the door had been, crashed into Helen and they both fell to the floor, she being trapped by his weight, all the breath knocked out of her. Pushing up and away from her, he sat glaring down at her with blazing blue eyes.

'Why on earth did you shut that door?' he roared at her.

'I . . . I. . . .' she gasped, drew a deep breath and sat up. 'I didn't know there was anyone outside,' she managed to get out at last.

He was there, actually there in the room with her. He wasn't a ghost but a handsome, vibrant man who didn't seem to be at all surprised to see her and who was furiously angry for some reason.

He was there with her, in the room where they had made love, and she wanted to touch him, stroke his cheeks, smooth his wind-ruffled hair, kiss the bad temper away from his eyes and lips, show him how glad she was to see him. Then she remembered the feeling she had had that someone was in the castle watching her. She remembered the creaking of a floorboard and a ghostly voice. 'Oh, it was you!' she accused. 'It was you all the time! You've been in the castle watching me. You . . . you enticed me to come into this room by . . . by pretending to be a ghost. Oh, you mischievous devil, you! I'm glad I closed the door on you—it served you right to be locked out there!'

Getting to her feet, she straightened her blouse and tucked it into the waistband of her pants. Magnus stood up too and went over to the dressing table to look at his reflection, while he smoothed his wind-ruffled hair back and at the same time to watch her reflection in the mirror, although she didn't know he was doing that.

'I didn't know you were here,' said Helen, more quietly. 'I was beginning to think there was no one here.'

'Really?' He turned to look at her. 'Then why have you come here?'

'I was invited to come by your mother. She wrote and asked me to come and stay with her for the weekend.'

'My mother?' he exclaimed, and laughed rather jeeringly as he turned back to the mirror. 'Oh, come on, Helen, you can do better than that, surely? You can come up with a better excuse than that for following me here. My mother is in the South of France right now, staying with friends. She hasn't been to Carroch all year.'

'I did *not* follow you here!' retorted Helen, her temper beginning to rise again and she glared at his back.

'No?' His tone was sarcastic.

'No. I don't chase after film stars, or rock groups or ... or any other kind of popular entertainer. I ... I'm not a groupie, or whatever it is you call that sort of person who hangs about everywhere you go.' She drew a deep shaky breath, then burst out, 'And I'm not like ... like that woman in Hollywood either. You won't find me committing suicide just because you ... you'd seduced me and then dumped me. I really didn't know you were here. ' She spun round towards the doorway. 'And I'm leaving now. I've no wish to stay with someone ... as cynical and warped as you are!'

'Eilidh, wait! I. . . .'

'No!'

She marched through the doorway. Everything wavered in front of her eyes, shapes distorted because she was seeing everything through the tears that had welled in her eyes. Disappointed and angry because this first meeting with Magnus since she had parted from him at the airport was not going as she had hoped it would, she went right down the stairs without looking back, but when she reached the kitchen she didn't snatch up her bag and stalk out through the back door as she had intended to do. Instead she paused by the table to stare down at the letter which still lay where she had left it, remembering belatedly that she couldn't leave the island unless Magnus himself took her to the mainland in the motorboat.

A sound at the doorway leading to the hall drew

her attention and she looked round. Magnus was standing in the doorway leaning with one shoulder against the jamb, his hands in the pockets of his jeans, and she noticed for the first time how tanned he was; tanned by a sun much warmer than the sun that shone in Scotland. His skin was an attractive teak brown and was shown off by the plain white shirt he was wearing, unbuttoned almost to the waist, its sleeves pushed up casually to the elbows. The tan made his eyes seem bluer than ever as he stared at him from under frowning brows.

'Who told you about Rachel?' he demanded abruptly.

'Rachel?' she queried, puzzled.

'Rachel Marsh, the woman who committed suicide. Did you read about it in a movie magazine? Because if you did, you read a distortion of the truth.' His voice grated bitterly.

'No, I didn't read about her. Wanda told me.'

'When?'

'When I took her clothes back to her in Glencross.'

'What did she tell you exactly?' he demanded, frowning even more fiercely.

'She ... she was telling me how glad she was that you'd gone to Rome because she and your mother had been worried about you staying on Carroch for so long. She said she'd told you about her problem with Blair to take your mind off your own trouble and I ... well, I asked her what trouble, and she told me about the woman you'd been friendly with in Hollywood who'd taken her own life and left a note more or less blaming you for the way she felt. She said that although it probably wasn't true and you weren't to blame for the woman's suicide you'd let it get to you and were behaving as if you were to blame by brooding over it and becoming a recluse here on Carroch,' Helen paused, then whispered, 'Was it true? Were you to blame, Magnus? Did you seduce that woman . . . Rachel . . . and then dump her?'

'No, I didn't,' he replied, and let out a long hissing breath. 'It's a long story,' he added, pushing away from the door jamb and coming over to the table, 'and not a very pretty one.' His glance flicked up from the letter to her face.

'I . . . I wish you'd tell me your version,' she whispered.

He stared at her for a few moments with narrowed eyes, obviously considering the pros and cons of telling her.

'Please, Magnus. I . . . I'd like to know.'

'All right,' he capitulated suddenly. 'But not like this. Not here, not standing here, staring at each other as if we're enemies.' He stepped towards her. 'Eilidh, I'm sorry for what happened upstairs and for what I said. I guess you're right and I am a mischievous devil. My sense of the dramatic tends to run away with me at times and I couldn't help leading you on up the stairs. I was hoping to lead you out to the battlements and surprise you there.'

'I really didn't know you were here,' she said again. 'I thought you were in Rome.'

'We had to stop shooting the scenes in Italy because of a strike of film technicians. We'll have to wait until the strike is over, and heaven knows when that will be. I came back to Scotland last Friday. I went to Glencross Hospital to see you and was told you were away on holiday.'

'Oh, I didn't know. No one told me,' Helen

muttered in suprise. 'Why did you go to the hospital? Why did you want to see me?'

'I just wanted to see if you were like I remembered you being.' His mouth curled in the half sweet, half malicious smile and his eyes glinted mockingly. 'You know, cool and sharp-tongued,' he added provocatively. He shrugged, his glance going to the letter on the table. 'But you weren't there, so I came on here. I didn't enjoy being here on my own over the weekend, so . . .' he paused and flicked the letter with a long forefinger. 'I wrote this and sent it to you, not my mother,' he said flatly. He looked at her again, but not apologetically. Mischief danced in his eyes.

She looked at the letter. Her suspicions that maybe Megan Scott-Murray hadn't written it had been right, then, but she had never expected Magnus to admit he had written it.

'But why? Why did you sign your mother's name?' she demanded.

'Because I was afraid you might refuse the invitation if I signed my own name. I was afraid you might think I was playing some sort of trick on you again by asking you to come and stay here with me, and me alone. I figured you were much more likely to come if you could be led to believe my mother would be here and that everything would be above board and sensible.' He grinned at her mockingly. 'And you did believe it. You fell for it and you came, Eilidh. You're here, and you're not leaving until I let you go.'

'Oh, you're mad, quite mad,' she retorted shakily, 'And you were wrong.'

'I was? How?' He frowned at her.

'You were wrong to think I wouldn't have come if you'd invited me yourself. I'd have come because

... because. ...' She broke off, suddenly shy because of the way he was looking at her, her glance faltering away from the expression of desire that blazed suddenly in his eyes.

'Go on, Eilidh,' he urged, stepping close to her. 'You'd have come because?'

'Because I've also been wanting to see you again,' she went on in a whisper, aware now of his closeness, of the warmth and scents of his body radiating out to her, encircling her, bewitching her. 'I wanted to find out if you ... if the man I met here in June ... was real. I'm here now ... I only accepted your mother's invitation because I thought she might be able to tell me something about you, tell me what you were doing.' Suddenly unable to stand the torture of being close to him but not touching him, she reached out and flung her arms about him and laid her head against his bare chest, hearing his heartbeat change rhythm, throb with excitement. 'Oh, Magnus, I've missed you so much. I've wanted to be with you. I've wanted to write to you. I've wanted to fly to Italy and find you.'

'Then why didn't you?' he whispered, his arms going around her. 'You'd have been most welcome, Eilidh. Every day when I finished work I wished you'd been there to help me unwind and relax.'

'I ... I was afraid you might think I was chasing you ... like other women have.' She raised her head to look at him accusingly. 'And you did think that, didn't you? You accused me of following you just now in the bedroom.'

'I know I did, and I've said I'm sorry. I said that to test you.' His lips twisted wryly. 'You see, Eilidh, I've never known a woman who liked me for myself, and even now it's hard to believe that I've at last met one who doesn't care that I'm a film star.' He smiled down at her. 'Upstairs you reacted as I hoped you would, but you're not leaving, Eilidh, are you? Not yet, anyway.'

'No, I'm not leaving . . . yet, because I've remembered I can't unless you take me over to the mainland,' she said teasingly. 'I'll have to stay, at least until Sunday afternoon.'

'Only until then?' He frowned at her.

'Yes. I'm a working woman, remember? I have to be back at the hospital on Monday morning. How long are you going to stay here?'

'Until the strike is over. I could come with you to Glencross on Monday . . . and stay with you there, if you would like that.'

'Oh yes, I would like that,' she said, smiling up at him, her eyes shining. 'But the flat is very small,' she added, thinking more practically. 'And there's only a single bed, and—well, you might get very bored during the daytime with nothing to do.' She paused and then made her sacrifice. 'I think it would be best if you stayed here and . . . and I came to stay with you again, next weekend.'

'Perhaps you're right,' he replied. 'There is something I have to finish while I'm here, a play I've been writing. But let's not make plans, Eilidh love. Let's just take it as it comes. You're here now and we're together for a while, so let's not waste a moment. "In delay there lies no plenty, Then come and kiss me, sweet and twenty, Youth's a stuff will not endure," ' he quoted, then began to laugh. 'Oh, Eilidh, do you think you could endure living with a man who's going to quote Shakespeare and other writers of plays in which he's acted to you every time he makes love to you?'

'Yes, I could endure it, as long as you mean what you say. Oh, please do it, Magnus, please kiss me. I've been longing for you to kiss me this past half-hour.'

'Then why the hell couldn't you have said so in the bedroom? Why did you have to rush down here?'

'There's always the lounge,' she whispered, linking her hands behind his neck and pressing herself against him.

'So there is,' he murmured, his eyes blazing with blue fire, and as his lips took hers he lifted her in his arms and carried her from the kitchen into the lounge, where they lay together on the sealskin rug.

Later, several hours later, when the sky was dark and pricked with stars, they walked along the beach in front of the castle, hand in hand, enjoying the soft mild air, while Magnus told her about the play he had been writing while he had stayed on Carroch in the months before he had met her.

'Wanda was right, I'd let the whole business of Rachel's death get to me, so I decided to write a play about it, as a sort of therapy, if you like, but also because I wanted to say something about the film industry and the awful and mostly false publicity which is put out about film celebrities and how sometimes it can destroy their lives,' he explained. 'I first met Rachel when I was a student at R.A.D.A. in London. She was older than me and a year or two ahead in her studies, but already a damned good actress destined to make a name for herself. Soon after she had appeared in a couple of plays on the London stage and had received rave reviews she went to Hollywood, made two or three films and then seemed to disappear.' He paused, then added slowly, 'When I went to Hollywood to act in films for Max Fiedler, she had a small part in one of them, but she had to be dropped.'

'Why?'

'She was always late and then she would forget her lines. Oh, it was awful to see what had happened to her!'

'Drugs?' Helen guessed.

'Right. I tried to help her and used to go and see her often, and of course our friendship was talked about, written about.' His voice rasped bitterly. 'But there was nothing in it. We weren't in love, we didn't sleep together and I didn't seduce her. That note she left was deliberately misunderstood by the coroner. I'd been away from Hollywood for a while, filming on location in the Caribbean, and she'd got very low because the man she was in love with, another actor, had married someone else.'

'What did the note say?' asked Helen.

'It was addressed to me and it said very briefly, "It's no use, Magnus, I can't go on without you. I'm going to finish it all tonight. All my love, Rachel."' He drew a sharp breath. 'Very misleading to anyone who didn't know the background to it, you have to admit.'

'She meant, I suppose, that she couldn't go on without your friendship and support, without you being there to help her,' said Helen, turning towards him, and they stopped walking to stand looking at each other in the starlight.

'Thank goodness you understand that, Eilidh,' Magnus whispered.

'Oh, it's very easy for me to understand, knowing how you rush in like a fool to help people,' she teased gently. 'How much more of the play do you have to write?'

'Only the last scene. I was trying to write it when Wanda turned up and told me about you and Blair and asked for my help. I haven't touched it since I enticed you here.' He framed her face with his hands. 'I really meant it, you know, when I said you'd come like a light into my life to lighten the darkness for me, Eilidh. I was very depressed after that farce of an inquiry into Rachel's death and the subsequent trial for slander, and I'd more or less made up my mind never to be in a film again. The problem was I was under contract to Fiedler and if I broke the contract was likely to be sued by him, something I couldn't afford to happen.'

'How long does your contract with him run?'

'This film—the one Leo is directing—should be the last. After that I'm going to freelance. I'll probably be very poor, but I'll be much happier only acting in plays and films when I want to, if I get any offers.'

'Oh, you'll get offers,' replied Helen encouragingly. 'I know you will. And then your play, the one you're writing, might be a huge success and your ego will get oversized again. . . .'

'Never, never while you're around to deflate it,' he retorted, and pulling her into his arms, kissed her hard on the lips. 'Oh, Eilidh, I love you very much,' he whispered when the kiss was over and he was holding her tightly, his cheek against her hair, 'What are we going to do about it? How can I always be sure you're going to be a part of my life and that I'm always going to be a part of yours? How can we be together more often when we do such different kinds of work?'

'We could always get married,' she said softly.

He was silent for a few moments, then he

pushed her away from him. In the starlight their faces were caricatures drawn in black and white, difficult to read.

'You wouldn't be proposing to me, would you, Helen Melrose?' he asked mockingly.

'Yes ... yes, I am, Magnus Scott,' she replied, 'because I know, you see, that you'll never propose to me. I love you too, and I want to be a part of your life and for you to be a part of mine always, and the only way I know we can make sure of that is for us to get married.'

'But that will mean making promises, Eilidh, and you know, because I've told you, I don't like to make them in case I have to break them,' he said quietly.

'If you love me, really and truly love me, you'll make them and you'll never break them,' she said.

'Do you want an answer now?' he asked.

'No. Just whenever you feel like it. We can go on as we are, seeing each other when we can,' she said. 'Shall we go in now? I think it's time we went to bed.'

'I *know* it's time we went to bed,' Magnus retorted, and sliding his arm around her waist he urged her towards the castle.

They parted from each other reluctantly on Sunday afternoon after arranging to see each other the following weekend. During the week Magnus phoned her from the Macleishes' cottage, just to make contact with her, he explained, to hear her voice and make sure she was still in Glencross, and she was able to tell him that she had managed to get Friday afternoon off so that she could drive to Carroch and they would be able to have two nights together at the castle instead of only one.

Promptly at noon, Helen left the laboratory to

walk to her car. All morning squalls of rain and wind had swept in from the sea and she wondered what it was like at Barracuish and if she would be able to cross the dangerous waters of the Carroch Strait to the island or if she would have to wait until the morning.

She fought her way against the wind around the corner of the hospital building and into the car-park, her head bent against the gusts. Only when she was near her car did she look up, and then her heart leapt. Someone was leaning against her car; someone in a yellow waterproof jacket, whose dark hair was wet and windblown.

'Magnus!' she gasped. 'How did you get here?'

'Archie was coming down to Glasgow, so I came with him and caught a bus from Glasgow to here.'

'Why didn't you come to the laboratory?' she asked, taking out her keys and unlocking one of the car doors.

'I wanted to surprise you,' he told her.

'Oh. Please get in the car,' she said, unlocking the door on the driver's side, 'or we'll get soaked.' Another squall of rain swept across the grey tarmac of the car park and hit the hospital building, rattling on roofs and windowpanes.

In the front of the little car they turned to each other and kissed long and greedily, holding each other closely.

'It was a wonderful surprise to see you,' Helen whispered. 'Oh, it's been an awful week, the longest I've ever known!'

'For me too,' Magnus replied. 'I had to come. I had to come and see you instead of you coming to see me. You see, I've decided I can't put up with not being sure of you. I can't go to Italy to make that film without being sure you'll be here for me to come back to. Eilidh, will you marry me?'

She stared at him, her eyes widening and beginning to shine.

'You mean it?' she whispered.

'I mean it. I've got to have some sort of commitment from you and I realise I can't possibly expect you to make a commitment to me unless I make a commitment to you, and that's what marriage is all about, isn't it?'

'Yes, that's what it's all about. Oh, yes, I'll marry you, Magnus. And thank you, thank you for asking me.' She slid her arms about his neck and kissed him gently and lovingly, because she guessed how hard it had been for him to decide on commitment.

'Then would you mind changing places,' he said when the kiss was over.

'What do you mean?'

'I'd like to drive so that we'll get to where we're going fast.'

'To Carroch?'

'No, not to Carroch. To wherever you parents live.'

'But why should we go there?'

'Because if we're going to do it, if we're going to be married, we're going to do it properly. I'm going to ask your father for your hand and we're going to be wed with all the trimmings. No half measures, Eilidh. No secret ceremonies. Agreed?'

'Agreed,' she replied, and hugged him fiercely. 'Oh, Magnus, I do love you!'

'So do I. Love me, I mean,' he said with a wicked glint. 'But I love you much more,' he added seriously. 'With all my heart. Now, how about changing places?'

Helen changed places willingly with him and the little car charged out of the car park at high speed, causing her to fasten her seatbelt hastily. Magnus was dangerous to know, and marriage to him wouldn't be always smooth and easy sailing. There would be many dangerous waters, full of whirlpools for her to navigate through, but being married to him would always be exciting and surprising. There would never be a dull moment.

A WORD ABOUT THE AUTHOR

Born in the port of Liverpool, England, Flora Kidd grew up to love the sea. She spent many hours with her father strolling the banks of the River Mersey, watching ships bring cargo from magic-sounding places.

While she attended university, her interest in sailing brought Flora into contact with her husband-to-be, Wilf, also a sailing enthusiast. After their marriage, he worked as a design engineer and she taught in a girls' school; from their combined earnings they saved...not for a home but for a sailing dinghy!

Eventually they moved to Scotland, where they lived in an old stone house on the Ayrshire coast. In those peaceful mountainous surroundings, with the Firth of Clyde in view, Flora began to think seriously about writing—and it wasn't long before her first novel, *Nurse at Rowanbank* (#1058), was accepted for publication.

Today the author and her family make their home in New Brunswick, one of Canada's Atlantic provinces. The Bay of Fundy has now joined the River Mersey and the Firth of Clyde as yet another maritime setting for Flora Kidd's delightful love stories.